Plus

Veronica Chambers

razor
bill

AN IMPRINT OF PENGUIN GROUP (USA) INC.

Plus

RAZORBILL

Published by the Penguin Group
Penguin Young Readers Group
345 Hudson Street, New York, New York 10014, U.S.A.
Penguin Group (USA) Inc., 375 Hudson Street, New York, New York 10014,
U.S.A.
Penguin Group (Canada), 90 Eglinton Avenue East, Suite 700, Toronto, Ontario,
Canada M4P 2Y3 (a division of Pearson Penguin Canada Inc.)
Penguin Books Ltd, 80 Strand, London WC2R 0RL, England
Penguin Ireland, 25 St Stephen's Green, Dublin 2, Ireland (a division of
Penguin Books Ltd)
Penguin Group (Australia), 250 Camberwell Road, Camberwell, Victoria 3124,
Australia (a division of Pearson Australia Group Pty Ltd)
Penguin Books India Pvt Ltd, 11 Community Centre, Panchsheel Park,
New Delhi – 110 017, India
Penguin Group (NZ), 67 Apollo Drive, Mairangi Bay, Auckland 1311,
New Zealand (a division of Pearson New Zealand Ltd)
Penguin Books (South Africa) (Pty) Ltd, 24 Sturdee Avenue, Rosebank,
Johannesburg 2196, South Africa

Penguin Books Ltd, Registered Offices: 80 Strand, London WC2R 0RL,
England

10 9 8 7 6 5 4 3 2 1

Library of Congress Cataloging-in-Publication Data is available

Printed in the United States of America

Plus

Meet Bee

This is the most important thing I've learned in my seventeen years on earth. Sometimes dreams change. Take, for example, my decision to enter the premed track at Columbia University. Being a doctor sounded all good and noble when I was sitting at home watching a special on TV about Doctors without Borders in Zimbabwe and imagining that in some small way I could change the world. But sitting in my dorm room, trying to remember the fundamental laws of kinematics, rotational dynamics, and oscillations, I'm pretty sure that I should've picked a different program.

I'm looking at the course catalog right now and I'm here to tell you that outside the world of geometrical optics, there's some pretty rocking stuff. If I hadn't been such a doofus and rushed into premed, I could be taking a class in "security, globalism, and terrorism." How cool would that be? I bet someone from that class will get recruited by the CIA to be a spy, like Jennifer Garner in *Alias*. I've rented the whole series on Netflix. Twice.

I should've been a spy. I would've been a really good spy because I can hear people whispering all the way across a room. My dad says I've got ears like a bat. He meant it as a compliment. But if you actually look at a picture of a bat, you might think different.

Unfortunately, I am not a spy. I'm a freshman Poindexter with a flat chest and size-ten feet. Everyone thinks I have a thing for capri pants, but it's just that I've got this defect where my legs are disproportionately long to the rest of my body, so my pants are never long enough. In junior high, they called me "stork legs," and there are still a couple of knuckleheads I see when I go home to visit my parents who'll yell out that inane nickname if they see me at Ben & Jerry's or in Rittenhouse Square.

I skipped a year of high school, so yeah, I'm pretty young to be a college freshman. But I'm what psychologists term an overachiever. I think the Latin term is *doae toomuchus*. If it weren't for my science-whiz skills, I'd be lost. It's pretty much the only thing that's always come easily to me. These days, even science is tough.

As my adviser, Professor Kelly (she's a psychology prof, and the one who diagnosed me as an overachiever), told me, I could've taken elementary physics (V-1202), or intro to mechanics and thermodynamics (C1401). But oh, no, that wasn't good enough for me. I had to prove I was a badass. I signed up for C2801, physics with differential and integral calculus, which required special permission from the instructor. Who was I trying to impress? I have no idea. I have three friends from high school, and they all went to college in California, so I see them like never.

The thing is, math and science were always so easy for me. I guess it's genetics: When you take a mama nerd and a papa nerd, they tend to give birth to a really geeked-out strain of super-nerd. My dad is a scientist at the Franklin Institute, a museum back in Philly. It's an egghead heaven, where you can walk into a giant human heart and see how it works or step into a chamber that simulates how it feels to walk on the moon. When I was a kid, there was a school trip to the Franklin Institute every year, and I always loved the way Dad would come out to the giant main lobby in his white lab coat, looking smart and kind and a little loopy, like he was the Wizard of Oz, like he had the answer to any question you might ever have—which most of the time he did.

Dad's been a big proponent of the grossology trend in science museums: meaning he creates exhibits about things like boogers and farts. It's a little too much for me, but Dad loves it. All you have to do is sneeze in front of him to get a twenty-minute speech on the wonders of snot. He's a funny guy. I guess in some ways, he's also the reason why I decided I wanted to become a doctor. I want to be the girl in the white lab coat, the one with all the answers.

My mom is an economist and does a lot of work with the World Bank. She's really involved with micro-loans to women in India and other developing countries. I guess the idea is that if you give a woman like a thousand dollars, she can buy fabric or goats or coconuts and make stuff she can sell in the market, and it helps her family and her whole community and creates some sort of sustainable economy. What this means in practical terms is that my mom refused to buy me a decent pair of jeans and I spent all three years of high school dressed in tribal outfits made by women in countries like Ghana and Peru. She refuses, I mean refuses, to buy anything in a real store since she claims that it's all made by underpaid child workers in third world countries.

So anything I've wanted, I've had to buy for myself. I tried to argue that giving a girl who does the dishes, cleans the guest bathroom, and takes out all the recycling FIVE DOLLARS A WEEK in allowance IN THE TWENTY-FIRST CENTURY makes me as exploited as a child laborer in China. But Mom just got even more mad at me and said, "And how much do you think they pay children to dig up land mines in Cambodia?" You'd think my dad would intercede, but he and my mom have this rule where they never contradict each other. I think the Latin term for this is *gangio upsa onihi daughterus*.

It took me nearly six months to save up enough money to buy a pair of jeans, and even then I was still wearing Mexican peasant blouses and hand-beaded moccasins every day. Honestly, it's gotten to the point where I kind of like my global village clothes. But it would be nice if my mom would take me on a trip to some of these places so when people go, "Nice poncho, where'd you get it?" I'd have some cool story about how I spent the summer in the Amazon instead of having to tell them my mom bought it at a fair-trade store in Washington, D.C.

But lest you think my life totally sucks: I should tell you that I have this hot boyfriend. His name is Brian Alexander. He's a sophomore, and he's like something out of a J. Crew catalog. I'm tall—around five nine, though honestly I've stopped measuring because I swear if I grow another inch, then the giraffe wranglers at the zoo are going to come and get me.

That's why it's extra nice that Brian is taller than me. He's six two, with this massive red hair, so you can always spot him in a crowd. He's got these adorable freckles and this smile that could melt butter. The thing is, he's such a good guy. I swear he'll probably be president of the United States one day. He's really into public service. Not in an annoying way like my mom, but in a cool way like Angelina Jolie and Brad Pitt.

I met Brian during frosh orientation when I went to a Blue Key meeting. Blue Key runs a lot of the charitable groups on campus like blood drives and the soup kitchen and all kinds of fund-raisers. Brian was giving the welcome talk, and since he's so good looking, he could read the telephone book and I'd find it fascinating. The talk he gave was superpowerful.

We were sitting in a room of about thirty students. I was at the back, helping myself to the free cookies, when I noticed him approaching the podium. He got up and said, "The summer after my freshman year, I traveled with the Red Cross to tsunami-affected villages in Tamil Nadu. It was a shock to me because of how I grew up—and what I was taught at school and was aware of—to see that there was a world with so much poverty and so much distress. We all hear about people fighting for clean water, fighting for shelter. The question is, is it charity to give it to them or is it a right? I joined Blue Key because I believe it's a right. It's not simply a question of being nice and helping with these things. It's not about good people doing nice things for desperate families. I disagree. Children should have an education. Children should have clean water. This is their right. It's not charity; it's human rights."

I wrote it down in my notebook in huge letters: IT'S NOT CHARITY; IT'S HUMAN RIGHTS.

I was staring at him, wondering what it would be like to kiss somebody so amazingly generous and kind. I flipped the page and I wrote:

Bee Alexander

Ms. Bee Wilson-Alexander

Mr. and Mrs. Wilson-Alexander

Then I noticed that the girl next to me was kind of looking over my shoulder, so I balled up the page with his name and put it in my bag to dispose of in a garbage can far, far away.

Brian told the group all about how he had met Bono at a benefit to raise awareness for debt relief in Africa. He'd organized three triathlons for spina bifida. Watching him, I thought, Wow, this is what college is about. I totally want to do cool stuff like benefits and triathlons. So I went up to him after his talk, determined not to freak out.

"Hi," I said. "That was a great speech."

"Thanks so much," he said, totally humblelike. "Tell me your name again?"

I hadn't even said my name, but the way he asked the question, it was like he was determined to remember it.

"Bee," I said. "I mean Beatrice. But my friends call me Bee."

He took my hand and held it, not in a nice-to-meet-you handshake, but in a sitting-in-a-movie-theater-on-a-first-date kind of way. "So pleased to meet you," he said.

"I totally want to join Blue Key," I said, sounding so *totally* like a dork.

"You should," Brian said. "Why don't you give me your number, and I'll call you sometime and tell you more about the work we do."

I didn't think he'd call. But he did, that same night. We went out for pierogies—delicious Polish dumplings—the following Saturday, and we've been dating ever since. Fall in New York City has got to be the most romantic time of year, and I lapped up every minute of it. I went with Brian to hear all these cool speakers at places like the Council on Foreign Relations. We went to see all these cool movies at the Film Forum, and then as it got colder we started swinging by Mariebelle after classes for hot chocolate. But the best thing of all was meeting Brian at this little diner near his house to read the Sunday paper, then taking long walks through Central Park, watching the leaves change and discussing all of the issues that were going on in the world.

It's been almost three months now, and I know people look at us and wonder how I snagged him. All I can think is that it's scientific. Take, for example, lightning. It's the result of one kind of charge in the clouds during a thunderstorm and an equal and opposite charge on earth at the same time. The two totally opposite charges meet together in space and neutralize as lightning.

Brian is really sweet. He's always saying that I'm beautiful and that my clumsiness is charming. But I think he's just being nice. My theory is that Brian and I are like lightning. My ultimate nerdiness and his ultimate hotness came together and manifested itself into one very electric kiss that sparked a whole relationship.

Bee Bops

Here's the deal. I'm not some kind of prude. But by the time I enrolled in college I was still a virgin, and I planned on staying that way for the foreseeable future. Maybe it's because my sophomore year of high school, Mason Riley, the girl who was class valedictorian, got pregnant. I didn't even know her, but like everybody else in school, I stared as she walked around the hallway, her belly getting bigger and bigger. By the time graduation rolled around, she looked like she was going to pop that puppy at any second.

There was a whole big flap because the principal didn't want her to give the valedictorian speech, but her parents threatened to sue, and so she gave this speech—the usual hoo-ha about working hard and dreaming big. But as I watched her, I thought, This is a girl who scored 2380 on the SATs. She *must've* been using birth control. For the first time, I believed the sex-ed hype. No type of birth control is infallible. Accidents happen. I'm a clumsy girl. There's only three steps at the front of our house, and I fall down them on the regular. I looked at Mason Riley's big old belly, and I didn't want the accident to happen to me.

That was all well and good in high school, when I went to the junior prom with this kid Max, whose parents have known my parents since college, when they all joined the Peace Corps. Max was cute, but our parents used to bathe us in the tub together until we were in like third grade, way past the point they should've stopped. So while it was really nice to make out with him on prom night, I think we both felt like it was practice for something bigger and better.

When Brian and I first started dating, I told him I was a virgin and he said it was cool. But he's nineteen; he'll be twenty in the spring. I can't expect him to wait around forever. So a couple of weeks ago, I went and got a prescription for the pill. Then I bought some condoms and kept them in my purse. And then just for good measure I visited the free clinic and got the patch. I left the doctor's office feeling very mature and sexy, like Lady Chatterley's lover. Or I guess, I mean like Lady Chatterley. You know what I mean. Mature. Sexy.

This past weekend, Brian's roommate went out of town, so he called and asked me if I wanted to sleep over. "Sure," I said, hanging up the phone and trying to be cool. But then I totally started freaking out. Everyone says I'm so lucky because I got a single dorm in the housing lottery, but these are the days when I think, yeah, right. I really wanted someone to talk to. I could've called one of my friends in Cali, Rebecca or Haylie or Rose, but I felt so awkward. There would have been this whole long catch-up about the weather and classes and folks from back home, when all I wanted to do was say, "Look, I think I'm going to have sex for the first time tonight, and I am SCARED OUT OF MY MIND." I looked at my cell, and it was like I had temporary paralysis. I could see the phone. I knew how to use the phone. But I was *not* going to pick it up and say those words. I just couldn't.

I decided that this sex conversation needed to be a face-to-face thing. So I put on my L. L. Bean jacket (it didn't contribute to the global economy, but my mom said it was okay because we bought it at a thrift store, so the environmental footprint is very small) and walked the ten blocks to my aunt Zo's house. Her real name is Zoe, which, as she's pointed out, is a name short enough not to warrant a nickname. But I've been calling her Zo since I was a kid, and she'll always be Zo to me.

Zo is cool. She's got this fab rent-controlled apartment on Central Park West, and she's a pit musician for shows on Broadway. She plays the upright bass, but for *The Lion King*, she plays all kinds of African string instruments too. When I was a kid, she did every show I ever wanted to see: *Grease* and *Into the Woods* and *Annie Get Your Gun*. Now

she's doing *Lion King*, and she says, "I'll probably be playing `Hakuna Matata' until the day I die." She loves the
show, and for a working musician, nothing beats a steady
gig. Whenever she takes me out to dinner or shopping and
I say, "Thanks, Zo," she always says, "Don't thank me.
Thank Uncle Disney."

Still, as much as I love her, as I walked down Broadway, I wasn't exactly relishing the idea of having the sex
convo with my mother's sister. But I figured I needed advice, and Zo loves to give advice.

When I got to her building, I rang the doorbell, but
there was no answer. I rang again; no answer. I don't know
why I didn't think of calling before I came over, but I guess
that was it. I wasn't thinking. Zo had given me a key, so I
let myself in and left her a note on the kitchen table. I considered writing some semblance of the truth:

Dear Aunt Zo,

*Came over to get advice about sex. You're not here, so I guess
I'll figure it out.*

Love,
Bee

But instead I just wrote:

Hey, Auntie Zo,

Where've you been? You never call, you never write. Why don't you treat your favorite starving niece to brunch sometime soon? I'm free on Sunday.

> *Love,*
> *Bee*

Then I put the frog paperweight she keeps on her desk on top of the note. Aunt Zo says she keeps Froggie around to remind her that in real life when you kiss a frog, it never turns into a prince. I gave the frog a kiss anyway. Maybe it would give me good luck.

I looked at my watch and realized I had just enough time to make it back to campus. I tutor this guy Kevin in math twice a week. It's a pretty good gig. He pays me twenty bucks an hour, and we usually work for about two hours at a time. All he's got to do is fulfill the basic science requirement, which this oddly counts toward. Everyone calls the class he's in "math for poets," but he acts like it's plotting vectors and orthogonal coordinate systems. I mean, really. But he's an aspiring rapper and supersweet, so it's fun to hang out with him. He says he's happy with a C and that I do a great job explaining everything. But I can't help but think that if I were a really good tutor, he'd manage to pull a B. Maybe that's just the overachiever in me speaking again.

I was halfway there when I noticed a Victoria's Secret store. I thought about the fact that I was wearing Snoopy Day of the Week panties—Friday, with Schroeder playing the piano and Lucy staring dreamily at him—and it occurred to me that I needed to step up my lingerie game. If I rushed, I would only be fifteen minutes late meeting Kevin. And Lord knows, he kept me waiting all the time.

Inside the store was like another world. Everything was pink and black and so grown-up. Not all of my panties have cartoon characters on them, but I didn't own a single piece of underwear that looked anything like this. Right away, some gorgeous blonde girl asked me if I needed help. Why? Why do people always ask you if you need help when you are trying so hard to be invisible? I'm pretty convinced that if I was ever in a situation when I actually needed help, like if a well of quicksand opened up in the asphalt on Amsterdam Avenue, not a single soul would ask me if they could be of service.

I thought I could grab something quick, but as Lenny Kravitz blared out of the speakers and I wandered from rack to rack, I grew more and more confused. There was a cute everyday bra-and-panty set, purple with cream ruffles, which could be a good choice. Make it seem like I wasn't trying too hard. But it was my first time; I wanted to look like I was trying, just a little bit. There was a whole section of garters and belts and corsets that looked more like torture devices than something you'd want to seduce your boyfriend with. There were long nighties, short nighties, camisoles, and tap pants. The music seemed to be getting louder and louder. Lenny Kravitz was singing, "Are you going to go my way?" and I just wanted to scream, "I don't know which way I want to go! Do I go 'girl next door' or 'ever so slightly slutty'? That's why I'm here in Victoria's Secret, trying to figure it out!"

In the honeymoon section, there were all these baby-doll nighties with matching robes. I looked at the price of the whole outfit and thought I must need glasses. This stuff was expensive. I've got a credit card, but my dad sees all the bills, and how was I going to explain a hundred-dollar charge at Victoria's Secret? I looked over in the corner and saw that they had these nice big fluffy bathrobes with matching slippers. That's what I'd tell him: bathrobe and slippers. And if I budgeted my meal plan super-carefully and saved some of my tutoring money, I could buy a robe and slippers before my parents' next visit.

I looked at my watch. I was now thirty minutes late for my tutoring session with Kevin. This is all I have to say: It's hard. On TV shows, they always make it seem so easy to be a teenage girl who's about to have sex. Even on stupid reality shows, the girls have nice hair and know how to do their makeup. They're always wearing the right kind of underwear, and they never look afraid. They look totally ready and into it, as if they are standing in line to ride a roller coaster at Six Flags. But that's not how I felt. I felt nervous and scared. My hair was totally flat, and I had no idea what to wear. I love Brian and I wanted him to be really impressed, just the same way he was impressed with

the fact that I'm premed and that even though he's a sophomore, I can help him cram for his organic chemistry exams.

I grabbed a red lacy night set, paid for it as quickly as I
could, then raced out the door. I knew that Kevin wouldn't
be waiting for me in the student center, but I went anyway
figuring that there was always a chance that he was even
later than I was.

When I got there, he was texting on his BlackBerry.
"What's up, little mama?" he asked.

Kevin is the only person in the world who would call a
giraffe of a girl like me "little mama."

"Sorry I'm late," I said, sitting next to him.

I took a whiff. I have no idea what kind of cologne, or
shampoo, or body lotion Kevin wears, but it's really delicious smelling. Clean, like green apples. But kind of pep-
pery too. I always want to ask him what he's got on, but
I try to keep things professional since I'm his tutor. I also
don't want to feed his already-massive ego.

The fact that Kevin is preternaturally good looking has
not escaped my attention. He's tall, with a short Afro and
the kind of square jaw that brings to mind old-fashioned
movie stars in the films that I watch with Zo. He also has
the most beautiful brown skin. He's like that Christina
Aguilera song "Lady Marmalade": Kevin is the epitome of
"mocha chocolate ya ya." The thing is, the fact that he's
good looking hasn't escaped Kevin's attention either. He's
always dressed to the nines. Today, he was wearing a kelly

green cashmere V-neck with a white shirt underneath and slate gray pleated pants. He never dresses like the other guys at school. He always looks like he's just stepped out of a Ralph Lauren ad.

"No problem, Bee," he said. "Why don't we just chill for a few minutes? You want a smoothie or something?"

I was starving like Marvin. "I'd love a smoothie," I said.

"I remember your drink. Strawberry, orange, banana with a femme boost," he said with a wink.

I could feel myself turning red. Maybe it was because I had sex on the brain. Or maybe it was the way Kevin winked at me. But the way he said "femme boost" made it sound much more sensual than what it actually is, which is a vitamin combo of calcium, iron, and folic acid.

Kevin went and got the smoothies: the usual for me, mango for him, and he came and sat back down.

"Hey, thanks for the drink. I'm sorry again about being late," I said. "Can we do a makeup session on Monday? I'll give you the hour for free."

He said, "What about tonight? I could take you to dinner."

Kevin's asked me out before, but I'm pretty sure that he asks a lot of girls out. Maybe that's why he always smells so good: It must be Eau de Player.

I smiled. "Sorry, I've got plans tonight."

Kevin looked down at the Victoria's Secret bag. "I see."

I blushed again and shoved the bag to the side with my

foot. "I needed a robe," I said.

He wasn't going to let me off the hook. "Tiny bag for a robe."

"Whatever," I said with a grin. "So what are you up to this weekend?"

"You know, I'm just gonna be in the studio, trying to get my rap thing going."

"Oh yeah," I said, laughing. "I thought you did your 'wrap thing' in the gift department at Macy's."

"So you got jokes," he said, smiling. He had a smile like a toothpaste commercial.

It was so easy to talk to Kevin. I'll tell you something I've never told another soul: Sometimes, just to keep up with Brian's conversation, I have to prep before I see him. I turn on CNN, listen to NPR podcasts, do a quick skim of the *New York Times*. Because if I'm talking to Brian and I don't know that Darfur is in Africa or what tribe was displaced in Sudan, he gives me this really pitiful look and says, "That's the problem with America. We think we're the center of the world." With Kevin, I may not discuss global issues, but I could be myself.

"So when do I get to hear this album that's going to the top of the charts?"

"At the album-release party next month. You're going to be there, right?"

"Oh yeah," I said, distracted. No way was I get-ting Brian to go to a hip-hop release party unless it was some kind of benefit.

"You should come hang out with me in the studio sometime," Kevin said.

"And be one of your groupies?" I said. "I don't think so. How many times do I have to tell you? Me, premed. You, flunking Math 101. We, plenty of work to do."

Kevin shook his head. "I know, I know. You don't even know how much pressure I'm under. The label doesn't even want me to be in school. I've got all kinds of things to do: interviews with *Vibe*, *King*, the *Root*, photo shoots, a track for DJ Clue's mix tape."

"I don't even know what half that stuff means," I said. "But if you have your degree, you'll have it forever. Don't you want to have something to fall back on?"

For the first time, Kevin looked really hurt. "Fall back on?"

"In case this music stuff doesn't work out," I said, slurping the last bit of my smoothie.

"You don't get it, do you?" Kevin said. He has this square jaw, which sometimes, when he's serious, makes him look like the sheriff in an old-fashioned western movie. "Music is my passion. I want a college degree because I want to be an educated person, but I'm not here to get a job. Music is my job. It's my life. There is no plan B."

I didn't know what to say. I really hadn't meant to hurt his feelings, and I was having such a good time hanging out with him that I'd forgotten all my stress about the big sex weekend again.

"I'm sorry, Kevin," I said. "I know your album's gonna be ridiculous."

"I don't need you to tell me that," he said, the tiniest smirk hinting at the side of his mouth. "I got ears. I know how good I sound when I'm on the mike."

"Well, that's a relief," I said, pretending to wipe imaginary perspiration from my forehead. "I was worried that for one second you might have doubted yourself."

"Never," he said, flashing his pearly whites. His Black-Berry started buzzing.

"You need to get that?"

He looked over the number and then turned the Black-Berry facedown. "I'll holla at them in a second. I'm wondering about you."

"What about me?"

"What's your passion, Bee? What do you think you can do better than anybody else? What do you love to do so much that you'd do it for free?"

Ooh, I thought. Now he's getting deep on me. But I didn't mind.

"Well," I said. "You know I want to be a doctor."

"Have you ever worked at a hospital before? Or is all this ambition based on marathon reruns of *Scrubs*?"

"No," I said sheepishly, because it was true, I kinda loved *Scrubs*.

"Then how do you know you're going to love medicine?

How do you know that's your passion?"

All of a sudden, the fact that I was good in math and science didn't seem to be enough.

"I gotta bounce, Bee," he said, standing up and giving me a little hug. "But think about it. When you say you want to be a doctor, are you really doing *you*?"

As I walked back to my apartment, Kevin's words stuck in my mind. Maybe before I dedicated the next seven years of my life to becoming a doctor, I should get some sort of internship to find out if this was really the job for me. Or maybe next semester I should sign up for that class on terrorism. Because I have to tell you, I could get pretty excited about being a spy.

3

Bee Stung

After hanging out with Kevin, I went back to my apartment to get ready. I was really glad I had that smoothie because I really, really can't cook. Sure, I've got a hot plate and microwave, but I don't know how to use bubkes.

I was about to take a shower and then I thought, You know what? This is my last night as a virgin. I should take a bath. So I poured a nice foaming bubble bath and settled in with an issue of *Cosmo* that I'd picked up especially for this occasion.

I took the red lingerie set out of the Victoria's Secret bag and wondered what exactly I was supposed to do with it. Should I put it on underneath my clothes and wear it over to Brian's? Should I carry it in a bag and change when I got there? I held up the red lacy panties and the baby-doll camisole and decided that the best thing to do was put them on underneath my clothes. I put the panties on. Itchy. But maybe it was like wearing heels for the first time. It feels a little uncomfortable, but you get used to it.

I put the babydoll nightie on, but none of the tops I had were long enough to cover it. I tried an oversize button-down shirt that used to belong to my dad. That worked, but it kind of creeped me out to be wearing my dad's shirt to go have sex for the first time. I tried my favorite V-necked sweater. Then a Columbia University sweatshirt. Finally, I decided to wear this old seventies wrap dress I'd found at a thrift store over my favorite pair of wide-legged jeans. I put on some high-heeled wedges, some mascara, eyeliner, and lip gloss. And I was good to go.

I was locking the front door when I remembered how good Kevin always smelled, and I turned back to spritz myself with some Sarah Jessica Parker perfume my aunt Zo had gotten me for Christmas.

The whole way over to Brian's, I was spazzing out. I had a toothbrush in my bag. A large box of condoms. Some spermicidal jelly. I was so scared about getting pregnant that I'd asked the campus doctor for the pill *and* the patch. She'd said no, that using both methods of birth control was going to make me sick. Not as sick as I'm going to be if I get knocked up, I thought. I took the prescription for the pill from the campus doc, then I made an appointment at a free clinic downtown and got the patch too. When I stopped to think about it, I did feel a little woozy. But I was pretty sure that it was just a bad case of the nerves.

Nothing bad was going to happen. I was only seventeen, but I was a freshman in college. Not to mention, I was in love. In love with a guy who was so smart and so committed to changing the world that he would probably end up running for office someday. He was worthy of my virginity. I was totally going to give it up.

When I got to Brian's apartment, he was as cute as ever. He wasn't dressed as fancy as Kevin was, but nobody dresses as fancy as Kevin. Brian was just wearing an old Coldplay T-shirt over a navy long-sleeve thermal tee and some jeans. He gave me a kiss, the kind of long kiss that I never understood before I went to college. When I was in high school and I saw kisses like that, I thought, Oh my God, what could they possibly be doing with their tongues for five whole minutes? Tongue calisthenics? Tongue push-ups? Counting each other's teeth with their tongues? But then I met Brian and I got it. With the right guy, a five-minute kiss is like a little slice of heaven.

I put my bag down and Brian looked at me and said, "You know nothing has to happen tonight."

I nodded and said, "But I want something to happen."

I said it, but deep down inside I didn't feel it. I loved him. I wanted to MARRY him. But on that particular night, I didn't want to sleep with him. But I didn't think I could say anything because it was all part of the love/marriage package. Somewhere in there, you had to start having sex.

He looked surprised. "Well, let's have dinner."

Brian's dad is a chef, so he's a really good cook. While almost everyone I knew at school subsisted on dining-hall food, ramen, and Chinese from Ollie's Noodle Shop, Brian actually made real meals.

"So what's for dinner tonight?" I asked, trying not to tug at the baby doll underneath my wrap dress.

"Risotto with mushrooms," he said. "It'll be ready in ten minutes. I've just got to keep stirring."

I sat down at the table and took a sip of the hard lemonade Brian had put out for me.

"Did you hear about the civil unrest in Basra?" Brian said. "It's just ridiculous that the secretary of state hasn't issued a statement. Doesn't it make you furious?"

"Mmm-hmm," I said, sipping the lemonade. I had no idea where Basra was, and I felt really bad about it. I have to say, it was a major catch-22 with Brian. On the one hand, he totally exposed me to the fact that the world is much bigger than I could've ever imagined and that there were so many causes that needed our help. On the other hand, it really was impossible to keep up. I know that he was planning on being a political science major, but still. How did he stay on the Dean's List and plan a dozen events a semester for Blue Key? I used to think I was smart, but Brian is way, way smarter.

He served the risotto in these beautiful handmade bowls that his parents had brought back from Italy for him. It tasted as good as it smelled. I, apparently, did not.

"Are you wearing perfume?" Brian asked, wrinkling his nose.

I was flustered. "Do you not like it?"

"Well, it's kinda strong," he said. "It's jamming my taste buds."

"I'm so sorry," I said, blinking back tears. This was supposed to be my big night, and I was feeling the opposite of the worldly girl I wanted to be. "Next time, I won't wear it."

Brian put his nose into his arm. "Could you go into the bathroom and try to rub some of it off with a washcloth?"

I was so shocked that the tears flooded my eyes before I could even stop them. I had put perfume on my wrists, but I'd also put it behind my neck, in between my breasts, and certain other unmentionable places. Was I really supposed to wash it all off? I was so confused. I stood up slowly, kind of hoping that he'd tell me that it was okay so we could just finish our dinner in peace.

"Just go," Brian said, laughing and waving me away with one arm as if I were a car blocking traffic.

Brian's kitchen is so tiny and I was crying so hard that I tripped over a box of pantry supplies his father had sent him. I tried to grab the table so I wouldn't fall, and both of our bowls came crashing to the floor.

Brian smiled halfheartedly and shook his head. "It's no big deal; I'll clean it up."

I was mortified. "I'm sorry, Brian," I said. "I'll pay for them."

"Don't worry about it," he muttered.

I walked through his apartment to the bathroom. He and his roommate had decorated it with all kinds of pictures of famous models and actresses. I knew that Brian's favorite picture was Bar Refaeli on the cover of the *Sports Illustrated* swimsuit issue. She was what he jokingly called "the TP"—the total package.

I took a washcloth from underneath the sink and washed off the perfume as best as I could. Then I looked at the picture of Bar. Okay, maybe I wasn't some hot Israeli model, but I wasn't a total washout. Even though I always complained about being flat-chested, I had filled out the babydoll top pretty well.

I took my wrap dress and jeans off. Then, after a quick deliberation, decided that I had to ditch the socks too. I did my best sexy walk back into the kitchen, determined to start my seduction over better. When Brian turned around to see me, the look on his face was the one I wanted to see.

"You look amazing," he said, coming over to me. He put one hand on my back to pull me closer, then kissed me.

"What about cleaning up the kitchen?" I asked.

"Forget about the kitchen," he said, kissing me again.

"What about the bowls?"

"Forget about the bowls."

"I'm sorry," I said again.

"Don't worry about it."

"Let me make it up to you," I said, hoping I sounded seductive.

He led me to his room, and we sat side by side on the edge of his bed.

I pulled off my top, revealing my sexy Victoria's Secret bra, and lay back on his bed. "Let's do this," I said.

Brian looked interested but surprised.

"Do you really think you're ready for this, Bee?" he asked, touching my chin so softly I thought my bones might melt and I'd turn into nothing but a pile of Silly Putty in his hands.

I took a deep breath. "Well," I said. "I've been on the pill for a month. I have a whole box of condoms. I also got a patch just for backup."

He laughed. "So you've been planning this for some time?"

"Of course!" I said. "I was thinking that maybe you could wear two condoms, though. Just to make sure."

Brian smiled, but now he was the one who looked uncomfortable.

"Don't you want to?" I asked, confused.

"Of course," he answered immediately. "I just wonder."

I could feel my heart pounding in my chest. And I was starting to feel dumpy in my red lingerie thing. What did he want me to say? One of the reasons I love math and science is that the answers may be hard to come by, but they're definite. I felt like Brian was asking me an essay question and only he could decide whether my answer was right or wrong.

"It's time to take our relationship to the next level," I said, trying to sound confident but feeling like my voice was getting squeakier by the minute. "You're nineteen. You'll be twenty in May."

I put my hand on his leg and inched it toward his privates. Then in a sexy whisper, I said, "A man like you must have needs."

His eyebrows shot up and he looked really disappointed, like he'd just turned on CNN and discovered that some warmonger from Bosnia had managed to escape prosecution from the international tribunal.

"You sound like you're quoting a magazine article, not something you actually feel," he said. "You're not ready for this, Bee. You're beautiful and you're smart, but you're just way too young for me."

"But I want you," I said, crying. "I want you so bad."

"I know," Brian said, pulling me close into a hug. "I know."

We pulled apart for a second, and he said, "You are so beautiful."

And all I could think was, Obviously not. Obviously I'm not beautiful enough to sleep with.

He stood up, went to his dresser, and pulled out a pair of pajamas.

"Put these on," he said. "Before I change my mind."

❈ ❈ ❈

I went into the bathroom to change, and it seemed like

all the pictures of girls in bikinis were mocking me. I wondered if when Brian was brushing his teeth, he heard the chorus of that old Pussycat Dolls song, "Don't Cha." He probably did.

He'd changed into another T-shirt and pajama bottoms. And we looked like two old people in our flannels as we crawled into his bed. We curled together like the letter *C*, and I couldn't help but feel how perfectly our bodies fit together. It wasn't how I'd pictured the night going, but it was so sweet just to be held by him. I slept better that night than I had in a really, really long time.

* * *

The next morning, I got up alone. Brian had already showered and was getting dressed.

"Hey there," I said, not moving any closer because I knew I probably had morning breath.

"How'd you sleep?" he said.

"Excellent," I said, with a big grin on my face.

"Good," he said, tucking his shirt into his pants. He came over to the bed and kissed me on the forehead.

"So, I should probably book my ticket to Chicago for Thanksgiving break," I said. Brian's folks live in Chicago, and he'd invited me home for the holidays weeks ago.

"About that, Bee…"

"Don't worry about the money. If I can't get a cheap ticket, my aunt Zo will give me some miles. She's got a gazillion."

"Bee," he said, sitting on the edge of the bed. "I think this is winding down."

"What?"

"We can still hang out and stuff. But I don't think we should play meet the parents over Thanksgiving."

"Oh," I said, getting dressed faster than I ever had in my entire life. "Okay. Cool."

"I'll see you around, okay?" Brian said as he kissed me on the cheek. Then he closed the door on me like I was some random person who'd rung his doorbell by accident.

4

Bee-Fuddled

I tried to wait until I got home to cry, but from the moment that Brian closed the door in my face, I could feel the tears coming and they just wouldn't stop. I ran home, I mean literally ran, and I know I must've looked crazy—I hadn't even combed my hair, and my face was all red and splotchy, and I could hardly breathe.

You know how sometimes you have a scary dream and no matter how hard you try, you can't get out of it? You think, If I can just wake up, everything will be okay. Well, that's what it was like the whole day after I left Brian's house. I was screaming and crying and trying to wake up. But I couldn't get out of it.

It would've been one thing if we had a big fight or if we disagreed about something huge. Like if I were a vegetarian and he kept insisting on eating burgers in front of me. But we didn't have those kind of problems. We didn't have any problems at all. It was perfect, and I couldn't believe he was punishing me like that: for something I did or something I said, when all I was trying to do was to make him happy.

I was crying so hard that I got a headache. Then I realized it was three P.M. and I hadn't had anything to eat all day. I went downstairs to the bodega and nothing looked good, so I just bought a little bit of everything: a bag of sour-cream-and-onion chips, a pack of powdered doughnuts, Snapple mango, some milk, a turkey sub, and a can of Chef Boyardee ravioli. I used to love Chef Boyardee ravioli when I was a kid, and even though I learned about all kinds of fancy Italian food, like risotto, from Brian, I don't have a thing against pasta from a can.

I analyzed every bit of the evening, everything he said and did, everything I said and did, and tried to figure out when I'd screwed up so badly that he wanted to break up with me. Like when I told him I wanted to have sex with him, I said, "I want you, I want you so bad." He hugged me and he said, "I know." But he never said that he wanted me, too.

I kept staring at the phone, hoping that Brian would call to apologize, even though I knew that he wouldn't. There was something so final in his voice when he said that this was "winding down." It was like on *America's Next Top Model* when Tyra sends a girl home. She has this really solemn look on her face, and she says, "Diedre/Claire/Barbara/whoever, you are no longer in the running to be America's Next Top Model. Please pack your things and go home." Sometimes, the girls cry and beg for a second chance, but the expression on Tyra's face never changes. On a gazillion cycles of the show, she never, ever changes her mind. That's the way Brian looked at me, and I knew that it was over.

I called my aunt Zo at home and on her cell, but it took her forever to call me back. When she finally did, I was so flustered I could barely speak.

"Bbbbbbbbrian bbbbrooke uuuup with meeeee," I sobbed into the phone. "IIIIII cccccalled yoooou HOURS ago . . . ."

Zo said, "I'm sorry, sweetie. I just got your messages. All fifteen of them, pumpkin. But I was at work. You know I have two performances on Saturdays."

Of course, I knew that. I'd just forgotten. I looked at the clock. It was eleven P.M. She'd just wrapped up the eight P.M. show.

"Do you want to come over and spend the night?" Zo asked.

"It's too late," I whined. "Everything's ruined."

"How about I take you to brunch tomorrow? I'll come by and get you about nine."

"Okay," I said, hanging up. I'd gone into that catatonic state where everything hurts so bad that all you want to do is sleep. But every time I closed my eyes, even if it was only for two seconds, Brian's sweet freckle face flashed before me, and I could feel myself aching to be with him all over again. It would've been one thing if back in September, I'd gone up to him at the Blue Key meeting and he never called and I just saw him at campus blood drives and Amnesty International fund-raisers. But we'd connected. We'd fallen in love. And I couldn't, for the life of me, figure when he'd fallen out.

* * *

The next morning, Aunt Zo picked me up for brunch. Sarabeth's on the Upper West Side. It's a fun place, always good for a celebrity sighting. Natalie Portman goes all the time and so does Drew Barrymore. We saw Julia Roberts once when she was doing a show on Broadway, and in the summer, when all these movie stars come to do Shakespeare in the park, you can barely keep your eyes in your head, the place is so full of famous people.

One morning, Zo and I saw this television news anchor who's known for being oh-so-serious and smart arrive at Sarabeth's on this big-ass motorcycle, all dressed in leather, with a girl not older than me on his arm. Aunt Zo said, in this really funny anchorperson voice, "Yet another tragic tale of male pattern baldness inciting midlife crisis. Story at eleven."

What really makes Sarabeth's so fabulous isn't the people; it's the food. All of it is so good, Aunt Zo said we should order like five things so we could taste everything. It's only when I think back on it do I realize how much I was packing away. (I did mention that Zo is an itty-bitty thing, right?)

Sarabeth's makes this awesome four-flowers juice. It's a blend of orange, pineapple, banana, and pomegranate. Aunt Zo had one. I had three. They call their hot porridge "Three Bears Style." I had a Mama Bear, which came with raisins, cream, and honey. Zo and I split the spinach-and-goat-cheese omelet. Zo had one square of the pumpkin waffles, so I finished them off. I also ate most of the chick-en-and-apple breakfast sausage.

"You know, Bee," Zo said. "There's not a single guy who ever broke up with me who didn't live to regret it."

I took a break from stuffing my piehole to let the wonder of that statement sink in.

"Are you serious, Zo?"

"Like a heart attack. Not all of them told me directly, but I heard about it eventually," Zo said.

I reached for another scone. I couldn't believe Zo was really going to try to placate me with the old "it's not you, it's him" argument.

"Are you hungry, Bee? Or hungry for love?" Zo looked concerned as I asked the waitress for another rasher of bacon.

All that psychobabble? That's so not Zo.

"Probably both," I said. "Come on, Zo. Stop talking like Dr. Phil and give me some news I can use."

She just sighed and said, "Relationships are about tim-ing, and being in college is like learning to play an instrument. For the first few years, your timing is all over the place."

This was, as she knew, not an empirical truth.

"My mom and dad met in college," I said. "They've been together for twenty-five years."

Zo shrugged. "There are exceptions to every rule."

I didn't say anything, but all I could think was, That's what I want. I want Brian and me to be the exceptions to this whole flaky college-dating rule.

* * *

The next day, I met Kevin at Starbucks for a makeup tutoring session. For like an hour before I saw him, I kept telling myself, "Don't cry. Don't cry." I even watched an episode of *How I Met Your Mother* on DVD, so that I could have something funny to think about if I felt the tears coming on.

I did all this prep work so I could keep it together. After all, I'd been crying pretty much nonstop for three whole days, but when I saw Kevin, I felt better. Not good, but better.

"So how was your hot date?" he asked when I walked over to the table where he was sitting.

"Don't ask," I said.

He pushed a cup toward me. "This is for you."

"What is it?" I asked, opening the lid.

"What's your favorite?" he asked.

"Caramel macchiato."

"Well, that's what it is." He smiled. "See? A brother pays attention."

You know how when someone's being so nice to you but it's not the person you want to be being nice to you? I kept wishing I was sitting with Brian and that Brian remembered all of my favorite drinks, which he never did, even when we were together and things were good.

"Well, thanks," I said. "But you don't have to buy me beverages, and I owe you for being so late on Friday. So this session is on me, and the next coffee is on me too."

We were working on Cantor's theory of sets, and for the first time, it seemed like he was really getting it. Maybe Kevin wasn't just a bonehead rapper after all.

"This isn't easy stuff; it gets into elements of trig," I said admiringly.

"I like it," he said. "It reminds me of hip hop."

"Oh yeah?" I asked, amused.

Then he started freestyling, right in the middle of Starbucks. I was kind of horrified at first, but then I saw just how good he was:

"There's an infinite set, just like there's an infinite us.
They tried to Jim Crow hip hop, but now we're driving the bus.
Bijunctive functions means you lay 'em out, don't count 'em out.
Kev's beats are hot, don't try to think it out, just twist and shout.
Bee'll sting you with the vectors and her axioms are maximum.
When my album drops, there'll be Grammys and more platinum."

Everyone in the coffee shop started to clap, and for the first time since the breakup, a whole hour went by and I hardly thought about Brian at all. Well, almost.

By the time I got back to my dorm, though, it was like someone had ripped off the Band-Aid. I missed Brian so much. As I was trying to decide whether I wanted to order Thai or Indian for dinner, I thought about how Kevin had talked to me about his music career. How he had asked me what my passion was. He'd said, What could I do better than anyone else? What made me feel so good that I wouldn't give up no matter what it took?

I placed an order for pad Thai, then broke out a bag of veggie chips to tide me over while I waited for dinner to arrive. I realized that while being a doctor is the profession I aspire to, it's not my passion. At least not yet. I'm seventeen; what do I know about healing the sick? What I do know is that I really, really love Brian. And I think I could be a better girlfriend to Brian than anyone else in this whole entire world. Winning Brian back is going to be my passion. Like Kevin said, when you're serious about what you love, there is no plan B.

5

Bee-reft

The next day, I woke up at noon and decided I was too devastated to go to class. I mean, I skipped a whole year of high school. Was I really going to get busted for taking a mental-health day? I ordered a pizza for lunch and then I wrote Brian a long letter, begging him to take me back. Then to make sure he got it, I walked over to his room and slipped it underneath his door. I mean in bona fide emergencies, can you really depend on the U.S. Postal Service?

I'm pretty sure he got it, but Brian never responded to my letter. I waited five whole days for him to call me, and then I thought, You know what, maybe the letter sounded too desperate. Maybe I just needed to *show* him what a horrific mistake he'd made by dumping me.

I thought about the way Aunt Zo said that eventually all of her exes came around. Maybe it was because Aunt Zo always looked so fabulous. Even though she's a pit musician and you never actually see her onstage, she's always dressed up.

Unlike my mother, who owns about eighteen copies of the same black dress and then piles each of them with tons of ethnic jewelry, all handmade by some worthy woman in an economically deprived part of the world, Aunt Zo can *really* dress. Like when we went out to brunch last Sunday, she was wearing a cute little leather jacket with race-car patches, a black T-shirt, a cool purple skirt, and these knee-high Gucci boots. The whole time we were in the restaurant, guys were checking her out. Even guys my age.

When I first introduced Brian to Zo, he said, "Damn, if you're going to look like that in twenty years, we ought to get married."

How could I have forgotten something as important as that?!!!!!?? BRIAN was the first person to bring up marriage, not me. I had to fix whatever was wrong, and I had to do it soon because I was losing my mind without him.

Maybe if Brian saw me in a high-fashion outfit like Aunt Zo's, he would change his mind. Maybe he didn't want to date a girl who wore Peruvian ponchos and Himalayan yoga pants. In an ideal world, I'd just go over to Aunt Zo's and borrow some of her clothes. But she's like a size six and I'm like a size twelve, a size ten if I suck in my gut and don't breathe.

Borrowing Zo's clothes wasn't going to work. But what about the credit card that my dad had given me for "reasonable expenses"? *Certainly*, buying myself some decent clothes was a reasonable expense. I could pretend that I had an interview for an internship and that while my three-piece Nigerian boubou was considered perfectly adequate for tribal high holy days, it wasn't going to cut it for a college student looking to intern at a major research hospital. That sounded like a feasible story, right? I mean, I planned on getting an internship at a major research hospital just as soon as I sorted out things with Brian and me.

So I went to Forever 21 and bought myself a funky print skirt, a fake leather jacket, and a pair of high-heeled boots. I liked the way I looked in the outfit, but I needed to step it up if I was going to get Brian to take me back.

Before attending a big event, like say the Tony Awards, Aunt Zo always goes to a department store and gets her makeup done. You have to buy some of the products they use, but chances are, you were going to buy some anyway.

I decided that this called for Bergdorf's. When I arrived I could hear Zo in my mind, telling me, "The Laura Mercier counter is good for a subtle French-girl look. Nars is good for shimmer, healthy, bronze-beauty stuff. And whatever you do, don't go to the MAC counter; those guys always manage to make women look like drag queens."

The woman at the counter was pretty. She had super-pale skin, jet black hair, and ruby red lips. It sounds extreme, but on her, it was ethereal, like she was a character in an old black-and-white movie. Her name was Françoise, and she spent an hour painting my eyes the shade of lilacs and my lips and cheeks in this beautiful lush shade of gold.

"You have amazing skin," Françoise said. "Did anyone ever tell you, you look like a younger Savannah Hughes?"

Yeah, like anyone would ever compare me to a super model. But by the time Françoise was done, it wasn't such a ridiculous idea. There was a big billboard of "Savannah for Sephora" near campus, and Françoise had re-created the look in the ad to a tee.

Although I knew my dad was going to kill me, I bought every product Françoise used—including a sixty-five-dollar bottle of "invisible foundation"—and paid for it with his credit card.

I took the subway back uptown and realized that Brian had his Arabic immersion class every day from three to five P.M. It was only four thirty. So I went to the coffee shop on the corner of his block.

Eva, the Hungarian waitress, handed me a menu.

"Where's your boyfriend?" she asked.

The question just slayed me. I kept telling myself, "Do not cry. Do not ruin your makeup. Do not cry. Do not ruin your makeup."

Even though I'd had a burger, fries, and a milk shake for lunch, I went ahead and ordered a piece of apple pie à la mode and a Coke. I mean, they weren't just going to let me sit in the coffee shop and drink water while I waited for Brian. And it was way too cold to wait outside.

While I polished off the pie, I went over my plan:

Go see Brian.

When he sees me looking gorgeous, he'll ask me to come home with him for Thanksgiving. I'll say that I'll think about it.

Play hard to get if he asks me to stay for dinner. Tell him I've got dinner plans. But maybe the next day.

❊ ❊ ❊

Aunt Zo is always saying that feminist revolution or no, it never hurts to play a little hard to get. It reminds people that you're valuable. Well, I wanted some of that. I wanted Brian to think I was more than valuable; I wanted him to think that I was *irreplaceable*. I had to prove to him that I was ready for the real thing. That I *am* mature. That I'm worthy of him.

❊ ❊ ❊

This is what actually happened:

I went to see Brian.

He said, "Wow, you look gorgeous."

I made out with him.

❊ ❊ ❊

About two hours later, he said, "I gotta get ready. I'm supposed to meet up with some guys to check out this band downtown."

"Great," I said, "I'll go with you."

"It's all the way downtown at Arlene's Grocery," he said. "I'm probably going to crash at my friend Ty's place. I don't want to have to worry about you on the subway."

"I'll just take a cab," I said.

Brian sighed. "Don't do this, Bee."

All of a sudden, I was sobbing again. "I thought you said we could still hang out."

He rolled his eyes. "I didn't say that. I mean, maybe I said that. But clearly you're too immature to deal with a casual thing. Come on, Bee. You have to go."

And for the second time in a week, Brian closed the door to his apartment right in my face.

* * *

The next day, I woke up feeling pathetic and sad. I wanted Brian back more than anything, but I needed to regroup first. I had grades to keep up, after all. My physics prof, Professor Trotter, was ruthless. So I walked over to Butler Library to get some studying done.

I was back on track and dreaming of allotropic forms when I saw Brian and some girl coming out of the library. Maybe he didn't even know her. Maybe he was just holding the door for her. But she was laughing, and he was smiling that charming smile. I ducked behind a column so he wouldn't see me. Then I turned around, ran down the steps, and hopped the subway to SoHo and walked to Mariebelle, where I had a giant hot chocolate and, instead of cracking open my lit textbook, read the latest issue of *InStyle* magazine. Welcome to "Life Post-Brian," in which our heroine (me, Bee) discovers that nothing douses the flames of heartache like a gallon or so of chocolate.

＊ ＊ ＊

A few days later, I was having lunch in the dining hall by myself when Brian came up to me. I thanked God that I'd washed my hair and put on a little eye shadow, despite the fact that I was still feeling miserable. But Brian wasn't in the mood to notice. He was really angry.

"Stop following me. I saw you at the library the other day," he said. His normally sweet, handsome face looked so . . . different.

"It—it was an accident, being there the same time that you were," I said, stammering. "I mean, I've got to go to the library and study. You don't own the building, you know."

But it was like Brian didn't hear me, and all of a sudden, I noticed that the tiny blonde girl he had been holding the door for at the library was standing off to the side, waiting for him while he told me off.

"First you show up at my house, then you follow me to the library. And don't think I don't know it's you calling my cell and hanging up."

Yes, I went to his house. Yes, I saw him at the library. But I wasn't calling him. I swear. I was so confused, it was all I could do not to break into tears on the spot.

"Someone's been calling my house and hanging up, Bee," he said. "The number is unpublished, but I know that it's you."

"I don't have an unpublished number. I don't even have a landline. My cell is a friends-and-family phone. It shows my dad's name. You know that."

Brian wasn't having it. "All I know is that you're the only person who is acting desperate enough to call me at all hours of the night," he said. "I need you to grow up. This happens all the time. Two people hang out for a while, one person grows out of the relationship and moves on. Stop making a federal case out of it."

He was speaking so loudly that everyone in the dining hall could hear him. I was so mortified. I just kept blinking wildly, like someone had sprayed mace in my eyes.

"It's over, and if you keep stalking me, I'm going to report you to campus security."

Then he stomped away. The boy who had been doing tongue calisthenics with me barely a week ago STOMPED AWAY.

At this point, I was nearly hyperventilating. I was breathing in and out so quickly, I thought I was about to have a heart attack, which is why I didn't notice this girl sit down across from me.

"You do know that he's a dick," she said.

"Who?" I asked. I was in a complete daze.

"Lyin' Brian. Two years ago, when we were both freshmen, he pulled the same mess with me."

"You used to go out with Brian?"

"Sorry to burst your bubble, snowflake," she said. "You're not in a club of one."

I looked down at my tray of fried chicken, mashed potatoes, and collard greens. For some reason, all of a sudden I was really, really hungry. So I started eating. I noticed that on her tray, the girl had a Caesar salad, an apple, and a bottle of water. Besides the fact that she used to date Brian, the goody-goody food on her plate only added to my instant dislike of her.

"So what do you want with me?" I asked.

"I kind of owe you one," the girl said. "I'm the one who's been calling Brian's house and hanging up."

SHE was the girl who was calling him and hanging up! Do you believe it? Do you believe me now when I say that my luck just goes from bad to worse?

"What? You've got to tell him." I had to get her to clear my name. Brian was never going to take me back if he thought I was stalking him.

"He ruined my freshman year, and I know that hang ups drive him crazy," the girl said. "So I call him nonstop for a few weeks, then I lay off and start up again. It really messes with his head." She burst into a big grin. I couldn't help but notice that she had nice teeth, pearly white and the kind of straightness that not even braces can produce, but at this particular moment, they looked more like fangs.

Will somebody PLEASE wake me from this nightmare? This nightmare where I am not only dumped by the love of my life, but I find myself having lunch with his psycho ex-girlfriend?

Granted, she didn't look like a psycho. She was this

really glammed-up Latina girl who looked a lot more like the posters in Brian's apartment than I did. But still.

"I'm Consuela. We should be friends," she said, putting her hand out for me to shake.

I did not want to shake this crazy girl's hand. Luckily, I had my greasy fried-chicken fingers to hold up as an excuse.

"I'm sorry," I said. "I just don't think I want to be friends with Brian's ex. Nothing personal."

"Well, I'll see you around," she said.

Then she flashed me this huge smile as if she were my new best friend. As if the idea of me being friends with someone who'd swapped spit with the love of my life were even *possible*. I think the Latin term for this is *movea onu crazae ladyil*.

As I walked home, all I could think was, This is just great. *I mean really great. Truly* great. I didn't mean it in a good way. Oh no. I meant it in the sarcastic opposite way. Brian thinks I'm stalking him, which I ABSOLUTELY am not. And now his psycho ex-girlfriend is going to be stalking me too.

Bee-friended

I was so freaked out by Brian confronting me in the cafeteria that I decided to avoid it entirely. I had no one to eat out with, so I ordered in. After a while, all the delivery guys knew me. And that, my friends, is how I gained the famous freshman fifteen—plus ten more, for good measure.

I don't know if you've ever been there, but being depressed is VERY TIRING work. I needed to eat for sustenance. It was like there was a great big hole inside of me, and it was sucking up everything: my ability to get out of bed, the energy it took to shower, the brain cells I needed to study. Eating, planning my meals, and going out for snacks kept me going.

I didn't want to see Brian in the dining hall, so I just relied on plastic for takeout and delivery. I used my card at the bodega, at Pathmark, at H&H Bagels, and of course at Ollie's Noodle Shop. It's not like I sat down and ate a whole pizza by myself in one sitting. But let's just say, when Dad got the credit card bill, the Victoria's Secret charge was going to be nothing compared to how much I was spending on food.

The thing is that I never felt overweight. The scale was creeping up, but I didn't feel fat. Six inches around your waist doesn't actually feel like a tire, no matter what the infomercials say. It feels like your belly goes from flat to soft, like every day is the day after Thanksgiving and someone has been stuffing your jeans with pillow feathers at night when you sleep.

I never wear panty hose, but I knew I was gaining weight when tights started being a problem. When you go to school in New York, a pair of warm wool tights can be your very best friends. My old tights wouldn't stay up. They kept slipping down around my butt, and I was always adjusting them. It wasn't until I was in the locker room at school and this girl saw me pulling them up around my thighs one day and said, "You might want to go up to the next size," did it occur to me that my legs—never toothpick thin to begin with—had taken on a greater proportion.

My face might have been chubbier, but I never noticed it. When I woke up in the morning, washed my face, and brushed my teeth, it was the same sleepy eyes that greeted me, the same crinkly smile when I heard Pharrell start to sing, "You're beautiful. And I love you. You're my favorite girl."

In high school, my teachers were constantly saying,

"You just wait until you get to college; all these silly distinctions and cliques will fall away." Then I got to college and found out that even at a brainiac school like Columbia, it's still a lot like high school. There's still the prettiest girl, the smartest girl, the most eccentric, and the most talented. I wanted to be the smartest or the prettiest or even just the weird chick who wore one sock as a fashion statement and did art installations involving Chia Pets. But that's just not me. I'm too weird to be cool but too vanilla to be weird in an interesting way.

Then when I met Brian, all of a sudden, I wasn't just this blob. I was his girlfriend, and together we did all kinds of cool things I'd never done before. But now he didn't want to see me anymore, and it was all because I was a virgin. If I were experienced, if I'd rocked that Victoria's Secret lingerie like a supermodel, shown him I know what I'm doing in a relationship, then I'd still have Brian and everything would be okay.

❀ ❀ ❀

I was waiting for the Ollie's delivery guy to show up at the gate. It was a weeknight, so it would probably be Dewei (yeah, I know too much). My cell phone rang, then rang again three times before I could pick it up. Definitely Dewei. But when I answered the call, it wasn't Dewei, it was Consuela. Brian's ex-girlfriend.

"Hey, *chica*, what's going on?" She said it as if she'd called a thousand times before.

"Hey," I said, a little shocked. "I'm waiting for my noodles."

"Yeah, I know, I grabbed them from the guy at the gate. Dewei's my man. Open your door."

I did, and she was standing there. As she entered, I stood there annoyed that she'd shown up but relieved she had my dinner.

What was I supposed to say to her? "You know when Brian kisses you, right behind your ear, and you feel like you're going to melt right on the spot, isn't that the best?" We had nothing, I mean *nothing*, to talk about. But here she was, and I had to admit that even though I guessed that she'd ridden into town on the crazy train, I was kinda happy for the company.

I walked over to the fridge and took out two diet sodas. "I'm fine," I said, offering her one.

"Nah, I never drink that diet stuff," she said.

I thought, Of course not. Consuela was curvy, but curvy thin, like Salma Hayek, which I think is the cruelest anatomical joke of all. How can someone have boobs and hips like Jessica Simpson and still fit into a size-six dress? It's like all the fat cells in their bodies automatically mutate to the right places.

"I came by because I'm going salsa dancing at the Copa. Want to come?"

"Uh, no," I said.

"Why not?"

What I should have said was, "Because you're a crazy

stalker girl." But instead, I said, "It's Tuesday night; I've got to study."

"Well, just come for an hour. It would be good for you to get out."

"I just ordered Chinese food."

"MSG, baby. It'll keep."

"Why are you being so insistent?"

"Because I told you, we should be friends."

"But you didn't tell me why."

"Just a feeling. Or maybe it's because even the delivery guy knows how sad and pathetic you are. You're definitely coming with me. Let's go look at your clothes."

"I haven't had any dinner. I'm hungry, Consuela," I said. I was whining like a baby, but I didn't care.

"First of all, everyone calls me Chela," she said. She took the bag of food away from me and looked inside. "You can't be this damn hungry," she said. She handed me an egg roll and left the rest of the food on the counter. "Eat this," she said.

"So now you're putting me on a diet?"

"Nah, Bee," Chela said. "I'm putting you on the clock. Ladies get in free before nine P.M., so we gotta roll. Where's your closet?"

I showed her.

She decisively reached for a black tank top and a red skirt. "Put these on," she said, tossing them at me. "You got some black pumps?"

I nodded.

"Good."

* * *

An hour later, we were on the dance floor. Chela said the old guys were the best ones to dance with and quickly found us a pair of grandpas. I was a little dubious of the five-foot-two man in the immaculately pressed black suit, but the minute we started dancing, he put one arm on my shoulder, one arm on the small of my back, and that was it. He made it seem like I'd been dancing salsa my entire life.

"Just follow me, *carina*," he said. "I'll take good care of you."

We danced song after song, until my forehead and back were dripping with sweat.

A couple of times, Chela caught my eye and winked at me. I couldn't remember the last time I'd had so much fun. But I also couldn't shake the fact that we'd both gone out with Brian and now we were hanging out. What was up with that? I didn't know exactly, but I knew that going out dancing was much better for my head and my hips than sitting at home crying about Brian and eating like there was no tomorrow.

* * *

The next day, I met Aunt Zo for a quick dinner at Joe Allen's. It was Wednesday, so she had a matinee performance that ended at five, then another performance at eight. I told her about how Consuela had come to my apartment and insisted that I go dancing with her. I told her about Adán, the old geezer that I danced with all night. And I told her how Consuela had been there when Brian told me off in the dining room and how she kept insisting that we be friends.

"Why is she so interested in me?"

Zo shrugged. "You're bright. You're beautiful. You're interesting."

"Spoken like a true auntie. I mean really, what's her angle?"

Zo said, "You know who you sound like right now, don't you?"

"Who?"

"Your mom."

I rolled my eyes.

"This is one of those moments, Bee," Zo said. "When you decide whether you're going to go through life with an open hand or a closed fist. What your mom did was look around and say, 'This is my life, this is everything I've got, and I'm going to hold on for dear life.' She holds on tight to everything she loves—me, you, your dad—but she doesn't realize that she's got a closed fist. Nothing can get out, but nothing can get in either. If you have an open hand, then people are going to take from you. People like Brian. But if you keep your hand open, it also means that people can give to you. People like Consuela. It's up to you."

* * *

Friday night, Chela and I hit the Copa again. She was dancing with a guy named Alejandro. He was cute, baby faced, dressed in a suit—which was kind of a nice touch, since most of the younger guys just wear slacks and button-down shirts. The guy I was with dancing told me his name was Quintan. He didn't speak a lot of English; he just kept whispering in my ear about how he wanted to *"toca su guitara."* When we left, Chela and Alejandro exchanged numbers. But I told Quintan that I didn't have one. A lame lie, but he got the picture.

Walking down Thirty-fourth Street to the subway, I asked Chela what *"toca la guitara"* meant.

She burst out laughing. "Is that what he said? Oh, Quintan had game!"

She explained that a woman's body, especially one like mine, is shaped like a guitar. She made an outline with her hands. *Tocar* means "to play."

"He wanted to play your guitar, *chica*," Chela said mischievously. "You know, that may be the way to get over Lyin' Brian once and for all."

"How's that?"

"There's an expression in Spanish: *Un clavo saco otro clavo.*"

"Meaning?"

"One nail takes out another." She made a slightly lewd gesture.

I rolled my eyes.

"You know, the best the way to get over someone is to get under someone."

"Oh yeah, that's not happening," I said.

"Why not?"

"Because I've got the goodies on lockdown till I graduate from med school."

Chela stopped in her tracks. "You're going to med school?"

"Well, not if I don't get it together on the grades front. But that's the plan."

Chela stood on the corner of Thirty-fourth and Eighth and smiled. "I'm going to med school."

"Get out!" I said, punching her on the arm.

"No, you get out!" she said.

We went back and forth with our "get outs!" for about five minutes.

We'd never actually talked about school. So far our conversations had been limited to Brian, boys, and salsa dancing.

"I'm going to be an OB, specializing in natural child-birth," Chela said.

I was impressed. "I want to be a pediatrician."

"I'll birth 'em. You'll keep 'em healthy," she said. "I told you we should be friends."

And just to prove that the stars were perfectly aligned, even though it was after midnight, we didn't have to wait two minutes before a local 1 train came pulling into the subway station, and we were on our way home.

On the subway, Chela turned to me and said, "Bee, I know it seems like I'm cool with the Brian stuff now. But when I found out he was cheating on me freshman year with some girl who worked at Beyond Borders, I nearly lost it big time. But I have to tell you, Brian's a boomerang. You can throw him away, but he always swings back. When he's between girlfriends, he'll call you because he can't bear to be by himself."

I was fighting to keep this stupid grin from creeping up on my face. Brian might actually call me? I might have a second chance at getting things right? I was so happy, I could've started doing the cha-cha right there in the subway car.

Luckily Chela didn't seem to notice. "He'll come back when he's bored or lonely, but he'll only dump you again, and trust me, it's going to hurt even more the second time."

I nodded. He wouldn't dump me again. The next time I went out with Brian, I'd know just what to say and do and wear. I was going to win him back, and this time, it was going to be for real. He was everything I wanted: someone cute, smart, who cared about the world, and was going to make a difference. He hadn't cheated on me like he cheated on Chela. He'd broken up with me because I'd been too immature. It was on me, not him.

"You know what they say, Bee," Chela said. "Men come and go, but homegirls are forever."

Is that what they say? Or is that what girls who've been dumped tell themselves so that they feel better?

"Let's make a pact," Chela said, putting out her pinkie finger. "We won't have anything to do with Lyin' Brian ever, ever again."

I reluctantly hooked pinkie fingers with Chela. Then I very subtly crossed my legs at the ankles so that God would know that I didn't really mean it. I liked Chela. Ever since I got to college, I'd been hoping to meet a friend like her: someone pretty and smart and fun that I could do crazy stuff like salsa dance with. But I also wanted Brian back in the worst way. I'd have to figure out some way to stay friends with her *and* be with Brian. Like Aunt Zo says, it's all a question of getting my timing right.

Are You Kidding Bee?

Chela and I started meeting for lunch almost every day. She worked part time at Balthazar, so we usually met downtown. That was cool with me; the farther away from Brian I was, the better. I was waiting for Chela at the Dean and DeLuca on Broadway and Prince when I saw this woman coming up to the counter. She was super-cool-looking, around forty, wearing a pink shearling coat, diamond-studded heels, and skinny dark blue jeans.

"I'm sorry, I'm saving this seat for somebody," I said.

"Did anyone ever tell you that you look a little like Savannah Hughes?"

She had this really fancy British accent, and even though I'd never heard the queen of England speak, I wouldn't be surprised if it sounded exactly like that.

I rolled my eyes. Yeah, right. Savannah Hughes was a big-time model, a supe. She used to be really skinny, then she almost went into cardiac arrest on diet pills and did the whole talk-show circuit about her eating disorder. A year later, she was back in the game as a plus-size model. She still got all the same bookings as before: *Glamour, Lucky, Domino*. I've got dark hair and full lips, but I look nothing, I mean nothing, like Savannah Hughes. That's like saying Rosie O'Donnell and Demi Moore look alike 'cause they have the same coloring.

But the woman wasn't going away. "Have you ever modeled before?"

I looked down at my chocolate-chip muffin and sub-consciously sucked in my stomach—no luck there. I was past the point of sucking my stomach in, unless there was a lipo hose involved. Who was this woman? And where did she get off making fun of *slightly* chubby girls?

"Look," she said, taking my silence for a no. "I'm a modeling agent, and I'm looking for a plus-size girl to star in the new Prada campaign."

I didn't know what to think. It seemed like that word—*plus-size*—was just hanging in the air like a flag made up of granny panties.

"It's a great campaign, very Sophia Loren meets *Roman Holiday*. Are you Italian?"

I shook my head.

"Can you ride a scooter?"

I shook my head.

"It doesn't matter. You're perfect for it. Call me, *today*. I've got to get this booked by Friday. Here's my card."

She handed me a card. LESLIE CHESTERFIELD, CREATIVE

DIRECTOR, CHESTERFIELD MODELING AGENCY. A phone number and an address on Bleecker. Then she walked out, and I still wasn't sure whether or not I'd just met my fairy godmother or I was being punked.

I was staring into space, trying to figure it out, when Chela came bursting through the door.

I handed her the card and said, "You'll never believe what just happened to me."

What I wanted to do was take the subway all the way up to 116th Street, lock the door of my room, and call Brian. Wouldn't he want me back in two seconds if he found out that some modeling agent wanted to hire me and had compared me to Savannah Hughes? I was just about to call him and try to drop the modeling news into the conversation ever so slightly when Chela showed up.

I love Chela, but it kind of sucks not being able to talk to her about Brian. It's like God is punishing me by giving me the coolest best friend, but to keep the friendship, I can't go anywhere near the guy I'm still in love with. I think the Latin term for this is *damnera ifae doit, damnera ifae dontas.*

"She's right around the corner, Bee," Chela said. "Let's just call her and find out if she can see you now."

I shivered involuntarily. "Maybe I should go to Bergdorf's and get my makeup done again. Or maybe I should run a few laps over to Chelsea Piers, see if I could lose a few ounces first."

Chela wasn't having it. "She knows what you look like

and she knows what size you are. She thinks you're gorgeous or she wouldn't have given you her card."

"At least, let me run into Zara and get something cute to put on," I said.

Chela shook her head. "You look cute. Like Nanook of the North."

I was wearing this Inuit parka that my mother had gotten me at some global village conference, jeans, and a pair of Ugg boots. I debated taking off my hand-beaded Navajo earrings, but I wasn't sure it would actually make a difference. I was so nervous. If I got an honest-to-goodness modeling gig, Brian might actually take me back.

"At least, let me run into Duane Reade and get some ChapStick. My lips are all cracked up from the cold," I begged Chela.

She reached into her bag and handed me her lip gloss. "Lip gloss is always cute on you."

I was about to say something about it not being hygienic, but I thought, What the hell?

I was staring out on Broadway when I noticed that Chela was now on her cell phone.

"Hello, may I speak to Leslie? This is Bee Wilson; Leslie gave me her card at Dean and DeLuca."

I tried to grab the phone, but she shooed me away.

"Okay, I'll be there in an hour. Should I wear anything special?"

Chela was quiet for a second.

"Okay. I'll see you then." She hung up the phone.

It was just like Chela to pretend to be me.

"What the duck?" I said, half mad and half relieved that she was taking charge.

Chela said that at her Catholic high school, all the girls said, "What the duck?" instead of the word that rhymed with it. I thought it was so funny that I had started copying her.

"Come on, Bee," Chela said with a big grin on her face. "Stop tripping."

"But you were pretending to be me."

"And? She just met you. She doesn't know your voice."

I simmered down. She was, of course, right.

"So what did she say?" I asked.

"You've got an appointment in an hour. No makeup, no new clothes. Just come as you are."

"An hour. That's plenty of time for me to at least get some cute shoes."

Chela looked more ready for a modeling shoot than I did. She was wearing this cool rasta cap and her jet black curls tumbled out just so. She had on a black ski jacket, skinny stovepipe jeans, and cool motorcycle boots. She looked at me and said, "I'm going to give you some advice, and one day, when you're a rich and famous doctor/ model/whatever, you're going to thank me. Do *you*. That's the only way you're going to get anywhere, be anybody, do anything. Don't worry about everybody else, just do *you*."

It was good advice. The only problem was, how could I

"do me" if I didn't even know who that was?

An hour later, we walked into Leslie's office, and it was like looking into one of those fun-house mirrors you see at the county fair. Every girl in there looked like me—some were fatter, some were skinnier, some were taller, and some were shorter. But we were all variations on the theme: vaguely ethnic-looking, pleasantly plump white girls with long dark hair.

"Do *me*?" I whispered to Chela.

"Just do *you*."

I walked over to the receptionist, who was this East Village punk girl and looked like the entire scene just bored her to pieces.

"Um, I'm Bee Wilson."

She nodded and wrote my name down. "Take a seat in the corner."

So I did and for an hour and a half, Chela and I just sat there as each girl was called into the back office, stayed for about ten minutes, and then walked back out.

I watched their expressions, and I began to feel like something terrible must be happening in that back room. One or two of the girls walked out with a big smile on her face, but most of the girls looked devastated afterward, as if they were trying not to cry.

I almost dashed out a dozen times. If Chela hadn't been there, I would've never stuck it out. But she kept me entertained with stories about her new guy, Alejandro.

"So did I tell you that he's been painting my portrait?" she said.

"That is so freaking romantic I could scream," I said.

She grinned. "I guess I'm a model too. Except when I pose for Alejandro, I have on a little less clothing than this gig calls for."

I raised an eyebrow; I'd been practicing how to do it since I was twelve. But it wasn't until I got to college that it started coming in handy.

"What does 'a little less' mean?" I asked.

"How about none?" Chela giggled.

"Get out!" I said it so loud that the snooty receptionist gave me a dirty look. Another girl exited the torture chamber, and then the receptionist called my name.

Chela squeezed my hand. "Do *you*," she whispered.

＊ ＊ ＊

Inside I found myself in a corner office, as big as a loft apartment, with two desks. Leslie was seated at the main one. Sitting on a gray velvet chaise lounge was a pretty Asian woman, older than me, younger than Leslie. She stood up and extended her hand. I shook it.

"I'm Caroline Kim," she said.

"Bee Wilson," I said, trying not to mumble. When I was little, I used to have a hard time articulating certain words, especially ones starting with the letter *s*. My aunt Zo made up this song—"I like to smile, and I like to smoke." For ages, I would sing, "I like to 'mile, and I like to 'moke."

I thought about it now because I felt like I was about to revert back into a five-year-old who can't say an *s* or anything else for that matter.

Leslie shook my hand. "I'm so glad you could come in. Sit down."

Caroline said, "So, Leslie discovered you at Dean and DeLuca's. How very Lana Turner at Schwab's."

"Who?" I asked. The question jumped out of my mouth before I could stop it.

Caroline just laughed. "How old are you, Bee?"

"Seventeen."

"What do you do?"

"I'm a student at Columbia."

Leslie smiled. "So you're smart. Miuccia Prada likes smart. What are you studying at Columbia?"

"I'm premed," I said. Not adding that I was going to be pre-Cinnabon employee of the month if I didn't get my act together and pull up my grades.

Caroline said, "Very impressive. So why do you want to be a model?"

I thought then of all the girls I'd seen who had left the office, fighting back tears. This must be where it all falls apart. They ask you a question. You give them the wrong answer, and they send you on your way. Somehow, I sensed that "I don't know. I never wanted to be a model" was the wrong answer. I thought about what Aunt Zo always said about her auditions: You've got to be hungry. You can't have a backup plan. So I just started making stuff up.

"I never see girls in ads that look like me," I said, which was true. "In my high school, they had to replace the plumbing in the girls' bathroom because so many girls were throwing up, the acid was actually eating away at the pipes."

This, as a matter of fact, was also true.

Leslie nodded. "So you're comfortable with your shape?"

"Absolutely," I said, semi-lying now.

"What if we needed you to lose a few pounds, just to tone up a little?" Caroline asked.

Again, another trick question. Was I supposed to stick to my guns, in a "fat is a feminist issue" kind of way? Or should I be flexible?

"I think exercise is good for everyone," I said. Then kicked myself. What must I have sounded like? A robotic candidate for Miss America?

Leslie stood up. "Let's Polaroid you, Bee." She took a camera off her desk, stood me against the wall.

I did a big old Kool-Aid smile.

Leslie said, "A little less teeth, Bee."

I turned it down a notch. She snapped my picture.

"Now closed mouth. Thoughtful."

I thought about Brian.

"Thoughtful happy, not thoughtful sad, Bee."

I thought about salsa dancing with Chela's friends at the Copa.

"Very pretty," Leslie said, and snapped my picture again.

Caroline said, "Now, let's see you walk."

I walked across the room.

I did it badly. I knew it right away from the look on Caroline and Leslie's faces.

"Can you try the walk again, Bee?" Caroline said. "This time, pretend that your favorite music is on."

"Don't be shy, Bee," Leslie said. "Pretend we're not even here. You're out with your friends on a Saturday night."

"Do *you*," Chela had said. But I knew at that moment, what I needed to do was Chela, strutting onto the dance floor at the Copa. I summoned all the South Bronx and South Philly I had ever seen and sashayed my hips as I walked across the room.

Leslie and Caroline were both smiling, but I couldn't tell if it was a real smile or a fake smile.

"That was really fun, Bee," Leslie said. "Thank you."

Then she looked down at her desk and started writing. I wasn't sure whether I should wait or leave.

"Should I go?" I said.

"We'll call you if we're interested," Caroline said. She was texting on her BlackBerry, and she didn't look up either.

❊ ❊ ❊

I walked out of the office, knowing now why some girls

looked like they wanted to cry. The whole "Don't call us, we'll call you" thing was pretty brutal.

Chela gave me a thumbs-up, then a thumbs-down. I just shrugged. We walked to the elevator in silence.

"You got the job?" she asked me once we were out on the street.

"I have no idea," I said.

"Did they give you any hints?" she said.

"Not a one. They said they'd call me if they were interested."

"Well, that sucks." She looked indignant.

I thought, She doesn't know the half of it. No modeling career, no Brian. Then I remembered how Brian had just about flipped when he found out that Shakira was a goodwill ambassador to the UN. Maybe if this whole modeling thing didn't work out, I could look into that. I mean, it wouldn't be just to get Brian back. I really believe in the issues, and as the Good Humor ice-cream man in my old neighborhood in Philadelphia can attest, I'm a girl who's just full of good humor, which is kind of like goodwill, right?

Bee-lieve It or Not

You know it's a good thing, a really good thing, that I wasn't born a gypsy and that I don't have to make my living telling fortunes like the girls you see with their crystal balls in little shops on Sixth Avenue. Because the truth is, I couldn't predict the future if my life depended on it. I thought Brian loved me and wanted to be with me forever. NOT. I thought I'd totally blown my modeling audition and that I'd never see or hear from Leslie Chesterfield again. NOT.

Leslie Chesterfield called me that *very same night* and asked me to come in the next day for another audition. I called Aunt Zo, and she said that this is what is known in show business as a "callback." Did I ever, in my whole entire life, or at least over the last three months when I was gaining weight like a polar bear getting ready for hibernation, ever think for a nanosecond that I'd be getting callbacks to be a model? NOT. NOT. And oh yeah, TRIPLE NOT.

* * *

I went back to the Chesterfield agency the next day, and there were only three of us in the waiting room. The stick-up-her-butt receptionist was slightly less disdainful. When I was called into Leslie's office, three other people were there—one woman, two men—sitting on chairs. Leslie and Caroline shook my hands but didn't introduce me to the new folks. I said hello to them, but they just kind of nodded. Caroline asked me to tell my name, age, and where I went to school. Then they asked me to walk again. I did my best Chela.

"Maybe a little less bounce," Leslie said, not smiling. She seemed friendlier the day before. Now she sounded exactly like the kind of icy society blonde that she looked like.

So I did it again.

Then Caroline said, "Thank you, Bee."

And it was over. So I said the only thing I could think of, which was, "Ciao."

Aunt Zo always said even when it's clear they're not going to hire you, always leave the audition with a smile on your face. Sometimes that's the only thing a conductor remembers, but it may be enough to get her to hire you for the next gig. So I smiled, said my "ciao," then went back to Dean and DeLuca for a jumbo chocolate-chip muffin.

I was sitting in the window when this cute guy stopped right in front of me. Then he made a brushing motion, and I thought, Great, some weirdo. He did it again, and I realized he was telling me I had chocolate on my face. I wiped it off with a napkin. He winked at me and kept walking. Memo to self: Next time I sit in the window seat at Dean and DeLuca, be in full makeup and sip a cup of green tea. My cell phone started to ring, and I knew that it was Chela calling for an update. Of course, I had to dig through my giant purse to find it. I thought I was so cool, rocking a fake Louis Vuitton bag to class instead of a knapsack, but this bag is like a pond: Everything sinks to the bottom and gets all scummy. Memo to self: Stop being so cheap and get one of those cute Japanese cell phone holders that clip on to the shoulder strap of the bag.

"Wassup, Chela. I blew it," I said when I finally found the phone.

"Hello, Bee?"

It wasn't Chela.

"This is Leslie Chesterfield. You didn't blow it. You've got the job."

I know. You totally saw this coming, right? But you have to understand. Things like this don't happen to me.

"Bee, are you there?"

"Uh, yes."

"Are you at Dean and DeLuca?"

"Uh, yes."

Now I was starting to get nervous. Were they spying on me? If she mentioned the chocolate-chip muffin, I was totally going to lose her number and forget all about this whole modeling thing.

"Great. Then maybe you can come over in about half an hour. We'll discuss all the details, and I'll draw up a contract."

I said okay, hung up the phone. Then called Chela. She wasn't there; I left a message. Feeling just a little bad for betraying our pact, I left a message for Brian and another for Aunt Zo. Desperate to speak to a real live person, I called my mom.

"Don't you have physics on Thursday afternoons?" my mother said.

Trust her to memorize my schedule.

"Mom, I'm being offered a modeling contract for Prada."

"Hmm, Prada," she said. "Let me do some research about where their factories are and how the World Bank assesses their manufacturing policies."

"Mom, do you even know what Prada is?"

She was quiet for a second, then she said, "They're not coming up in my database. Maybe I'm not spelling it correctly."

"I'm hanging up now, Mom."

Which I did. Which tells you everything you need to know about my mother and why Columbia is not nearly far away enough from Philadelphia to spare me from her misery. I did get into Stanford. I could've gone there, I thought as I tried very daintily to finish my chocolate-chip muffin.

I pulled out my phone and called my dad at his office.

"Dad, I got a modeling contract."

"A part-time job at a department store? That's great, Bee. Your grandmother used to go see the models at Wanamaker's. I think they served sandwiches."

"No, Dad, it's not that kind of modeling. This is for a photo shoot. I think it's going to be in a magazine or something."

"Well, that's great, Bee."

"Thanks, Dad."

"I've got a meeting next Tuesday at the Museum of Natural History next week. Can I buy my best girl lunch?"

"Absolutely."

"You know I always told you that *B* stood for 'beautiful.'"

Which is true. I liked to joke that the *B* in my name stood for "below average," but my dad always says the same thing, "I call you Bee 'cause you're beautiful." Which tells you everything you need to know about Dad.

In high school, I knew this really rich girl named Siohbahn. Her mother had done something really incredible, like invented the BlackBerry. Anytime someone asked her a question like how much her boots cost or if it was expensive to go skiing at Vail, she always said that it was "gauche" to talk about money. Aunt Zo says only people who actually have money think talking about it is so déclassé. This is all to say that I'm going to give it to you straight. I don't give a rip if it's gauche or déclassé.

I walked into Leslie's office, and she told me that they were booking me for three days at "five a day." She said, "It's not much, I know. But you've never done this before, so you don't have a quote. Hell, you don't even have a portfolio. Technically, the advertising agency is taking a big chance on you. But the upside is that while the money is low, the perks are high. The shoot is in Italy. They'll fly you business class and put you up for four nights at the Villa d'Este."

All this time, I'm thinking the free trip is cool. But these people want to pay me five dollars a day. If I wanted five dollars a day, I could've stayed at home and done household chores for my mother, who, not for nothing, is not too busy for third-world causes but is too busy to take out her own recycling. So I decided to try to negotiate. "Can I bring a friend?" I asked.

Leslie looked seriously bothered. "Bee, this is a business trip, not a social trip. It's very important that you don't get that confused. Everyone thinks that modeling is so glamorous, but as you'll soon discover, it's really hard work."

This is the point where I should've just shut up, but I figured, what did I have to lose? "But if you're only going to pay me five a day. . . " I said.

Leslie smiled. "I think I can get seven. Which after commission means you still clear more than twenty."

Okay, Bee, I thought, you're good at math. They

couldn't possibly mean seven dollars a day. They must mean seven hundred a day. But seven hundred a day for a three-day shoot is a little more than two thousand dollars. That's a lot of money, especially for someone who'd never modeled before.

I looked down at the contract and saw all the zeros and then it hit me. "Five" was five thousand. A day. American. And I'd just negotiated my way up to "seven," which was seven thousand. A day. American.

"Cool," I said, trying to play it off as if I made that kind of cheddar all the time, when in reality they were going to pay me half of my tuition for three days' work. I took a deep breath and said, "Where do I sign?"

* * *

I walked all the way from Bleecker Street in SoHo to my dorm. I passed a gazillion stores, and I kept wanting to run in and buy something. It was freezing cold, but I didn't feel a thing. I was rich! I was filthy, stinking rich! I didn't have to worry about charging that stuff from Victoria's Secret, Laura Mercier, and Forever 21 on my dad's card. I could pay him back.

Seven thousand dollars a day. Three-day shoot. One day of travel on either end. I got paid for those days too. That was thirty-five thousand dollars. The agency took 15 percent and Leslie said I'd have to put a third away for taxes, but still. I'd clear twenty thousand dollars for five days' worth of work. No wonder rich people thought it was gauche to talk about money. I didn't tell a soul. Could not get the words—twenty thousand dollars—to come out of my mouth.

At Fifty-ninth Street, I decided to walk through the park. Central Park is the best place in New York to go when it's cold and snowy. It's always packed, like an urban Disneyland—full of kids and people sledding and ice- skating. I even saw this guy on cross-country skis once. I thought about going to Italy: flying business class, staying at a fancy hotel. It sucked that I couldn't bring a friend, but it was worth a try. Leslie had said that with the money I earned, I could "take my boyfriend to Puerto Rico."

Maybe that's what I would do. When I did the job and showed Brian the magazine, he would take me back, and I could invite him on a romantic weekend getaway to Puerto Rico. I wouldn't even have to tell Chela until I was sure that Brian and I were completely solid. If things worked out with us, she wouldn't get mad at me. She was my friend, and your friends always want what's best for you, right?

* * *

The next day, I went to see my adviser. She said that she couldn't excuse me from a week's worth of classes but that students with professional careers were not uncommon at Columbia. She said that I needed to go to each of my professors, explain that I had a job in Italy, and ask if they could please give me the course work to complete in advance. This was fine with everyone, except for my physics prof, Petra Trotter.

I'm not just saying this because physics is kicking my ass. Prof Trotter is a strange bird. She's Canadian, which means she speaks English perfectly fine, but she says things like "aboot" instead of "about." She also grew up in the wilderness of Canada, which she talks about all the time, like it's the reason she's a math genius. Actually, her childhood in the wilds of Canada is the reason she's such a freak. She's always making faces, weird, exaggerated faces like the kind you make behind someone's back or when you're mimicking an animal at the zoo. Case in point:

I said, "Professor Trotter, I've got a job in Italy and I need to be gone from Monday through Friday of next week."

Professor Trotter scrunched up her mouth and sniffed, like she smelled something terrible or she was a baboon at feeding time. "Well, what's that aboot, eh?"

I said, "I'm going to miss two of your lectures next week and was hoping that you'd give me the assignments in advance. I know I only got a B on the last quiz, but I'm going to hire a tutor as soon as I get back from Italy."

She rolled her eyes and let out a big exaggerated sigh. "But that's a little like a Band-Aid on a gunshot wound, isn't it?"

A few FYIs:

One, there's no way in Hades I'm not going to Italy.

Two, I would hardly call a 3.2 average a "gunshot wound." It's a B. It's not great if you're on the major track, like I am. But it's not that far off, and I'm going to fix things.

"Well, Professor, what do you suggest I do?"

Her mouth twitched from side to side. She raised an eyebrow. She threw both hands in the air. The woman was incredible, like some sort of fanatical mime. After a few more facial tics, she said, "Well, you'd do well to skip the job and come to class, wouldn't you?"

I took a deep breath and then told the itsy bitsiest of lies. "Professor Trotter, I have to take this job in Italy. It's my only source of income, and I have to work as much as possible if I want to be able to come to Columbia next year. This is a very expensive school."

That made a dent. She shrugged. She puffed up both cheeks, then moved the air around from cheek to cheek. Then finally, *finally* she gave me the assignment.

As I walked out the door, she said, "It's a crying shame when students have to work instead of concentrate on their education, isn't it? But what are you going to do? It's a money-driven society, eh?"

Little did she know, I wasn't doing this for the money. Not really. I was doing it for Brian. Wait till he saw *me*, modeling in some high-fashion magazine. I knew I had this goofy cat-with-a-mouthful-of-canary look on my face, but I couldn't help it. I was going to get Brian back. I was going to Italy on a modeling job, and I didn't even have to humiliate myself on *Top Model* to do it. My life was officially on the up and up.

9

Bee Takes Flight

Did I mention that the closest I'd ever been to Europe was the It's a Small World After All ride at Disney World? I could hardly tell what geeked me out more: the fact that I was about to go on my first modeling job or the fact that I was headed to Italy. If the Chesterfield agency hadn't sent a car to pick me up and take me to the airport, I would've never made my flight. I would've gotten on the subway and instead of taking the train to JFK, I would've ended up at Yankee Stadium. I swear. I'm not wrapped too tight these days.

Then they flew me business class. Well, on Alitalia, they called it "executive class." Ha! I'm not an executive. I'm a seventeen-year-old freshman who got really, really lucky in Dean and DeLuca.

Aunt Zo warned me to pass on the free champagne they give out on international flights and not just because I'm underage. "It flows like water up there, and you don't want to arrive at your first job drunk," she said. But I made myself completely happy with OJ, the gnocchi that came on a real plate with real silverware, and the cannoli they served for dessert.

When we landed, I was met at the gate by a woman named Giovanna from the advertising agency in Milan. She looked more like a model than I did. Tall, thin, movie-star hair and movie-star sunglasses. She kissed me on both cheeks and said, *"Benvenuto, bella."* Giovanna had a porter get my bags, then she led me through customs. Since I was there for work, we didn't wait in a single line. Giovanna just spoke Italian rapidly and we stormed through.

A navy blue Mercedes was waiting for us, along with a driver who was so handsome that for the first time in months, I completely forgot about Brian. He drove us to the Villa d'Este. And what can I say? It's not a hotel; it's an *experience.*

First of all, it's not really a hotel; it's a castle, sitting on this beautiful lake. When you walk in, it's like a museum: stone walls, sculptures, paintings, Persian rugs. You take this winding staircase, like the one in Daddy Warbucks's house in *Annie*, up to your room. My suite looked out onto the lake and had a private swimming pool. (Giovanna insisted it wasn't a swimming pool; it was just a big Jacuzzi.)

It was heaven. Over dinner, Giovanna told me the whole story. The villa was built in 1568, which is way too long ago for me to even imagine. Then it was owned by a ballerina, one of Napoleon's generals, then an Italian

princessa and a Russian empress. It became a hotel in 1873.
She also told me that George Clooney owns a house nearby
and that he's always hanging out at the bar with his friends,
people like Matt Damon and Brad Pitt. I begged, like a
dog, to go to the bar after dinner. But we had a five A.M.
wake-up call the next day. Giovanna said, "You are the
model. You must rest."

"What if I want to make a call?" I asked. "Can I call
long distance on the phone in my room?"

Giovanna laughed. "You are staying at the Villa D'Este,
the most exquisite hotel in all of northern Italy. Of course,
you can call long distance."

I was so excited that I filled the gigantic bubble bath
with water. I got in, and then because there was a phone
right next to the Jacuzzi, I called Chela.

"Hey, Chela, guess where I'm calling you from?" I said.

"Italy, girl, I know," she said. "Tell me all about it."

"Where exactly in Italy am I?" I pressed.

"I have no idea."

"I'm in my very own mega-Jacuzzi! Can you believe
it?!!" I screeched.

"Get out!" she said.

"No, *you* get out!" I said.

We went back and forth that way for about five minutes because that's what we always do.

"This Jacuzzi is gigantic, Chela," I said. "You could fit
like six people in here easy."

"Why didn't you ask them if you could bring a friend?" she whined.

"I did," I said. "I TOTALLY did. But Leslie said it was unprofessional."

"Well, that sucks," she said.

"Tell me about it," I said.

I was so amped about the photo shoot the next day that I talked to Chela until the water in the Jacuzzi was ice cold and my skin was all dried up like the papayas in my mother's favorite trail mix.

When I finally hung up and got into my pajamas, I couldn't believe the time. It was two o'clock in the morning! I had to be up at five. I called down to the front desk for a wake-up call and then went right to sleep. No biggie, I thought. I'm a college student. I get by on three hours of sleep all the time.

* * *

I don't know what happened. Maybe the guy at the front desk *"no parle inglese"* the way he said he did. Or maybe the phone rang with my wake-up call, and I totally slept through it. It's been known to happen. But I overslept, and when I did pick up the phone, it was Leslie Chesterfield's very angry voice on the other end.

"Bee, where the hell are you?" she said. She wasn't screaming, but she had the kind of voice that could bring the pain without raising a single decibel.

"Hi, I mean, good morning," I mumbled. I was so, so

sleepy. I guess asking if I could hit the snooze button was out of the question.

"Do you know what time it is?" Leslie sniped.

"Five A.M.?" I said hopefully.

"It is six A.M. The photographer, the stylist, the makeup and hair people are all waiting for you in the lobby and have been waiting for over an hour. You do know this is unacceptable."

"But I thought my call was at five A.M.," I said. "How could I be an hour late already?"

She took a deep breath and then sighed. It was the indignant sigh of a very smart person having to explain something very simple to someone who was extraordinarily stupid. I knew it well because it was the same indignant sigh that my mother made every time I asked her why we couldn't buy our clothes from the mall like everyone else.

"Beatrice," Leslie said, reverting to my full name. "A five A.M. call means that you are ready to work at five A.M. This means you are in the lobby of the hotel, dressed, and ready for transportation to take you to the site of the shoot. In order to make a five A.M. call, you must then be awake by four A.M., earlier if you are the sort of person who drags in the morning."

Up at four A.M.? I know they were paying me the big bucks, but was she kidding me?

"Have I made myself perfectly clear?" Leslie asked.

"Um, okay," I said.

Then for about five seconds, her tone softened. "I understand that this is your first shoot. And it's entirely possible that some of the blame for your irresponsibility lies on my shoulders for not explaining the protocol to you. But this is not a business that deals in second chances, Bee. You've got to figure out where you need to be, when you need to be there, and then help the photographer create images that will satisfy the client. It's work, not play. You're a smart girl. I expect you to pick up quickly."

And then without saying good-bye, she hung up the phone.

* * *

I was so rattled that I wasn't sure I had time to shower. I flew out of bed, stepped into my jeans, and raced to the lobby, combing my hair with my fingers.

Dexter Haven, the photographer, was British like Leslie. He was one of those guys who tries to pretend he doesn't know how cute he is, but he can't quite hide it, kind of like Justin Timberlake.

Dexter had three assistants. They told me their names but then never really spoke to me again. They were too busy hopping to it every time Dexter needed a lens or a filter or a soda. There was a stylist, who also had three assistants. And there was a makeup artist, Syreeta, who, as it happened, was from Philly, so we had a million things to talk about. The hairstylist, Andy, was funny — very dramatic, very much the artiste, and very bald. He assured me, though, "The fact that I'm not worrying about my hair means that I can concentrate on yours."

We all piled into a really fancy minivan and drove about an hour to a beautiful little country town. That first day, I rode a bicycle down a hill for six hours. I kid you not. I rode it down the hill, laughing and smiling and trying to hold my hands above my head. Then one of Dexter's assistants would walk the bike back up the hill. It was a cool bike, a classic red Raleigh. I wore these beautiful sundresses—some were strapless, some had more of a halter top—and Syreeta dusted gold powder on my eyes, my cheeks, and in the middle of my cleavage. "Those puppies are the real stars of the show," she said, referring to my breasts. Hilarious.

It was fun riding the bike, but Dexter kept saying, "More in the face, Bee. More in the face." I was laughing and smiling the whole time I was on the bike, but I guess laughing in real life isn't the same as laughing so they can capture it on film. Every time Dexter took a break to show me the digital shots on his laptop, nine out of ten of them looked like I was about to be examined by a dentist, not like I'd been smiling or laughing at all.

Dexter was really nice about it. At the end of the day, he said, "It's okay; it's your first shoot. And we've got a couple of really gorgeous shots. Just try to remember, you're a model, so you've got to learn how to control your face."

I went back to the hotel and tried to make happy faces that didn't show off a bird's-eye view of my tonsils, but it was actually harder than it looked. After about an hour, my face really, really hurt, and I still wasn't sure that I was doing it right.

Leslie Chesterfield called at seven P.M., right before I was about to hop into bed.

"Bee," she said, her crisp British accent making it sound like she was going to keep me after school for detention. "I understand there's some problem with the face shots."

I was lying in the gigantic hotel bed, and I just wanted to crawl underneath the covers and never come out. I only had one face. I'd been smiling the same way my whole life. What was I supposed to do?

"Bee?" Leslie said. "This is modeling, not curing cancer. Just try to smile in a fashion that does not suggest that you are trying to catch flies."

"Okay," I said.

"Very well," Leslie said. "Good night, and remember that there are a hundred girls who would kill to take your place. *Apply yourself*, Bee, and set multiple alarms."

* * *

I knew what it meant to work hard at physics or calculus, but I had NO idea what it meant to "apply myself" as a model. I had always liked having my picture taken. My dad is a typical science geek, and cameras are some of his favorite gadgets. Maybe if they would hire my dad to take the pictures, I could do a better job. Somehow, I sensed that wasn't going to happen.

At the airport, I'd bought a copy of *Elle* with Savannah Hughes on the cover. I opened up the magazine and studied her eight-page fashion spread. I noticed that she never actually smiled in any of the photographs. Instead she did this cocky little smirk, and the left side of her mouth was raised ever so slightly as if she had a secret that was hers and hers alone.

I jumped out of the bed and went to the mirror in the massive marble bathroom. I practiced doing the Savannah smirk, and I'm not trying to brag or anything, but it looked pretty damn good.

Okay, I thought as I crawled back into the bed. Didn't both Leslie and the girl at the Laura Mercier counter say I kind of reminded them of Savannah? Tomorrow, I was going to work the Savannah smirk like no one but Savannah herself had ever worked it before.

Chela wouldn't approve. Her motto in life was "Do *you.*" But I'd tried all day to "do me" and the word had come from on high: When I was myself, I pretty much sucked.

❖ ❖ ❖

The next morning, I rode in a speedboat with a gorgeous Italian male model who didn't speak a word of English. He said a bunch of things I didn't understand, then Giovanna translated. "His name is Lucho. He wants you to know that he is gay, but he thinks you are very beautiful. Touch him anywhere."

What? She laughed and then demonstrated. She put an arm around his shoulders, kissed him on the cheek. "You are a couple in love," she said. "Lucho wants you to feel comfortable touching him."

All righty, then.

Dexter and the team rode in a boat in front of us, and Lucho and I were in our own boat. Peter, one of Dexter's assistants, lay down on the deck of the boat. He had a walkie-talkie and gave us all of Dexter's orders since we couldn't hear him over the crashing waves.

"Dexter wants Bee to hug Lucho," Peter said. "Dexter wants Bee to lean against the mast and close her eyes."

Then it was, "Dexter wants Bee to close her eyes and look thoughtful happy, not thoughtful sad."

It was funny to get these wacko instructions; it was kind of a mix between playing Simon says and being a life-size Ken and Barbie.

The good news was that Dexter was much happier with my smile. "Big improvement in the face," he said when we stopped for a lunch break. "It's a very sly, knowing smile. I really like it."

It was a long day, from six A.M. until sunset. I must've changed clothes thirty times. And after every meal, Syreeta had me wash my face so she could do my makeup completely from scratch. "We don't want you to get drag rot, girlfriend." I went back to the villa exhausted. But I would not, could not, with good conscience, call it work.

On the last day of shooting, Giovanna told me to sleep during the day. It was a night shoot, and we would work until three or four o'clock in the morning. The car picked me up at four P.M. We drove to another, smaller villa on the lake. Giovanna said it belonged to Giorgio Armani, who sometimes rented it out. I was surprised when I got there to find it was packed with people. Maybe fifty people were there, in addition to our usual dirty dozen.

"Extras," Giovanna said dismissively. "We are shooting a dinner party."

"That's a lot of people to have over to dinner," I said.

"This is how we do it in Italy," Giovanna said.

The clothes for this shoot were fancier, honest-to-goodness ball gowns with long poofy skirts. Andy said, "We're going the whole *principessa* route," and he put extensions in my hair so that I'd have curls going down my back.

I had a new "boyfriend" for this shoot, Marco. Although I received the same set of instructions: Marco was gay. He thought I was very beautiful. Touch him anywhere.

I kept thinking about Brian during the shoot. How I wished we were still together. How cool it would've been to take this amazing trip with him. How I wished instead of caressing Marco's extremely well-sculpted biceps, my arms were wrapped around Brian.

It was the last setup of the evening when I heard what sounded like gunshots. Dexter explained that we were all to go to the shutters, open them, and walk through the balcony doors onto the lawn. So we did. And when I looked up, I saw fireworks.

"Just like that, Bee," Dexter said, circling me as his assistants flashed strobes and bright lights in my face. "Look surprised. Look up at the sky as if you can't believe what you are seeing. That's very good. Excellent."

He showed me the images on his laptop, and there were a couple that were so good, I could hardly believe they were of me.

"These are the pictures I've been trying to get for three whole days. Look at those eyes," Dexter said. "*That* is the face of a supe. You can't manufacture that kind of magic. You look like a modern-day Alice in Wonderland."

It wasn't hard to smile at the camera like a girl who'd wandered into a fairy tale. I was at a villa, on a lake, in Italy, wearing a one-of-a-kind hand-painted ball gown. I was surrounded by beautiful people, I was being fed the most amazing food, and the sky was exploding with color. The awe Dexter saw in my face was absolutely and categorically real.

10

Bee in Hives

After I got back from Italy, I went in for a meeting with Leslie Chesterfield. I don't know why, but I half expected her to get up and kiss me on both cheeks, like all the modeling people I'd met in Italy. But she wasn't in a kissy-kissy mood.

In front of her was a big stack of photographs; all of them were of me. I was kinda stoked. I mean, she must've called me in to congratulate me for rocking the house on the Italy shoot, right? Didn't the photographer say that the last shots were perfect?

But when I went to her office, she said, "You've got to do better than this, Bee. There are a few shots here that are nothing short of amazing. But there are a lot of shots that look like they were taken for your yearbook. You've got to learn how to connect with the camera. A really great model knows how to bring something fresh to every frame."

Leslie's office was all white: white desk, white bookcases, white plush chairs, with funky pieces of sea coral on the bookshelves that matched the reddish orange telephone and rug. It had a cool kind of aquarium feel the last time I'd been in to sign my contract, but now, I couldn't help but see the ocean theme as a sign that I was sunk.

To the left of Leslie's desk was a flat-screen TV that was connected to her laptop. Every time she clicked her mouse pad, a picture of me came up.

It was a little embarrassing. One after another, a dozen shots of me on the bike came up on the screen. Every single picture looked like a medical photograph of someone being prepped for a tonsillectomy. The last shot was really pretty. I had a nice smile, and I didn't look gigantic in the clothes. I just looked like a curvy girl out for a bike ride on a perfect spring day.

"That one's pretty good," I said hopefully.

Leslie clucked and said, "My point exactly. One good shot out of a day's worth of film. If I were the client, I wouldn't book you again."

Doesn't that sound kinda harsh? Trust me, it sounds worse when you're hearing it from a rail-thin British woman with a razor-sharp tongue. Out of Leslie's pursed lips, the words "I wouldn't book you again" sounded an awful lot like "Off with her head!"

"Day two of the shoot," she said, putting up a picture on the flat screen of me on the speedboat with the male model Lucho.

"He was cute," I said, trying to make conversation. But

Leslie didn't say a word. She was too busy studying the photograph as if she were a scientist trying to identify a rare strain of the Ebola virus.

"The smile is better here," she said. "But what is wrong with your eyes? For heaven's sake, why are you wincing in this photograph?"

The way she said, "For heaven's sake, why are you wincing in this photograph?" had this, "*My God*, not in civilized society!" tone to it. Almost like when you're on the subway and you see a drunk, homeless guy taking a leak onto the track.

"Well, I think the sun was in my eyes," I said.

She pulled out a picture of Carolyn Murphy in *Vogue*, holding a surfboard on the beach. "Do you see her eyes?" she asked. "The way they are engaged totally in the camera? Do you know how she achieved this feat of physical prowess?"

I shrugged. "Maybe she wore tinted contacts?"

Leslie looked as if she was about to lose it. Big time. "No, no, no," she said. "When the sun is in your eyes, you turn your head. You turn your whole body if you have to. Your eyes are your most important tool as a model. It's more important than your smile. You've got to engage the camera with your eyes and then move your body accordingly. I'm going to have to add movement lessons to your schedule."

Movement lessons? I knew how to move. And what

schedule was she talking about? "Do you mean, my class schedule?" I asked. "'Cause I can't; I'm taking eighteen credits as it is."

"We will discuss your schedule after I'm finished with your portfolio critique," Leslie said.

You know it sounds all good when some woman walks up to you in Dean and DeLuca and asks you if you want to be a model. Then you get a business-class ticket to Italy, and they pay you a bunch of money. But when you come home and you have to sit in an office with said fancy-pants British woman and she puts picture after picture of you up on a big-screen TV to tell you how much you suck, well. . . It's like my kindergarten teacher used to say, "It's all fun and games until someone loses an eye." I really wished Leslie would stop poking me in the eye.

"What on earth was going on here?" she asked.

I looked at the photo on the screen. I was supposed to put my arms around Lucho's chest, but there was a big wave of water coming right at us. I was kind of crouching behind him, and all you could see were two scared eyes, my arms holding on for dear life, and some not-so-flattering shots of my jelly belly.

"Another boat was going by really fast, and I totally got splashed."

Leslie took out a stainless steel letter opener, and I wondered for a second if she was going to throw it like a dart at the screen or me.

"There are all kinds of problems in this photograph," she said. "Your eyes are like a dead fish's. Your jaw, what we can see of it, is clenched. Your arms are locked. And the rolls around your stomach are extremely unattractive."

Now, I was getting cranky. It was one thing for me to notice my own jelly belly; I didn't need to sit in this life-size aquarium and let Leslie Chesterfield feed off of me like a shark.

"Fine, then, I guess I should go," I said, reaching for my fake Louis Vuitton. I looked at my watch. It was two P.M. In an hour, Chela would just be finishing her shift at Balthazar. There was a free basket of pomme frites (that's French for french fries. Hilarious, right?) and a Coca-Cola with my name on it if I could get out of this torture session and get myself over there.

"Even thin models sometimes have cellulite," Leslie said. "It's a fact of female life. But every single model worth her salt learns to pose in a way that accentuates her attributes and masks her flaws."

At this point, I just wanted to scream, "You try it! You try being a wardrobe-challenged, big-boned beanpole whose absolutely perfect boyfriend just dumped her. I never said I was a model, lady, you did. I can't mask my flaws because there are too many. I can't play up my 'attributes' because I don't have any! I just want to go and eat french fries with my best friend in peace!"

I wanted to say all of that; I really did. But I have this

genuine medical condition in which I think up all this great stuff but never have the actual courage to say it.

So what I actually said was a really lame, squeaky, "I'm sorry."

"Don't be sorry, Bee," Leslie said. "Do better or I'll be forced to drop you from the roster."

I could feel my palms getting sweaty. It was one thing if I quit, if I walked out of the door in the pursuit of life, liberty, and french fries. But I really couldn't handle failure when it was being doled out by an authority figure. Take, for example, physics. I may complain about the absolute inanity of signing up for advanced physics. But even I know that a B is not failing and that if Professor Trotman would cut me just the tiniest bit of slack, I could pull it up to a B+ by the end of the semester.

A week ago, I'd never even thought about modeling. I'd never heard of the Chesterfield agency, and I had no burning desire to go to Italy. But now that I'd had a taste of it, I couldn't bear to give it up. I mean, I skipped a year of high school and got into the premed program at an Ivy League university. Certainly, *certainly*, I could learn how to smile so I didn't look like a horse.

"Are you serious about wanting to be a model?" Leslie asked.

"I'm *very* serious," I said. And all of a sudden, I really meant it.

"Then I need you to devote yourself to this fully," Leslie

said. "I don't want to ask you to drop out of college just yet. Although if things go as well as I'm hoping, then we might have to revisit this conversation."

Yeah, right, I thought. Drop out of college to volunteer in the Sudan? No problem. Drop out of college to be a fashion model? My Peace Corps–loving mom would jujitsu my butt.

"I've asked Caroline to print out a copy of your new agenda," Leslie said, handing me a piece of paper.

I looked at it.

"How'd you get my class schedule?" I asked, dumbfounded at the reach of Leslie's superpowers.

She looked bored. "I'm your employer. I simply had Caroline call the registrar and request it."

I could not believe this woman! "You can't just call the registrar's office at Columbia and request my schedule," I said. "That's totally illegal. You could be a stalker or something."

Leslie gave me her best Dr. Evil smile. "Caroline can be *very* persuasive."

I was kinda freaked, but I had to keep my eyes on the prize: Become a model. Get Brian back. Become a model. Get Brian back.

<u>Weekly Agenda for Bee Wilson, Chesterfield Models</u>
<u>12+ Division</u>

<u>Mondays, Wednesdays, Fridays</u>
6 A.M. to 7 A.M. Personal trainer, Sistrunk Fitness, Columbus Circle
10 A.M. to 4 P.M. Go sees/shoots
6 P.M. to 9 P.M. History of Western Music: Middle Ages
to the Baroque [Core requirement; I figured I might as
well knock it out early.]

<u>Tuesdays, Thursdays</u>
6 A.M. to 7 A.M. Personal trainer
8:15 A.M. to 10:15 A.M. Advanced physics
10:30 A.M. to 11:15 A.M. Phys-ed requirement: lap swim
11 A.M. to 12:30 P.M. Swahili
[Side note: I signed up for Swahili to impress my mother, champion of oppressed people everywhere. Was she
impressed? Not really. All she did was give me a lecture
about how Swahili is the lingua franca of East Africa and
the only African language spoken in the African League of
Nations. Do the words "Good job, Bee" mean anything to
her? I mean would it kill her to say *"nzuri"* or something?]
1:00 P.M. to 2:30 P.M. American Modernists
3 P.M. to 6 P.M. Frontiers of Science

I was a little shocked, seeing as Leslie's "agenda" left

me no room at all for studying, eating, or, most important of all, chillaxing.

"But I normally have physics from 2:00 P.M. to 4:00 on Mondays, Wednesdays, and Fridays," I said.

Who could possibly expect me to wrap my mind around quantum mechanics at eight in the morning?!! Leslie Chesterfield, that's who. I mean, yes, she runs a big, powerful modeling agency. And, yes, she knows all of these fancy fashion designers. And, yes, she has this perfectly waved golden blonde hair and always wears the most adorable shoes. But has Leslie Chesterfield ever tried to analyze the Rydberg constant before her first cup of morning coffee? I don't think so.

"We've taken the liberty of changing your schedule to accommodate go sees and shoot days," Leslie said.

Did you hear that? They've "taken the liberty" to change my course schedule. Doesn't that violate my privacy? Has the registrar at Columbia never heard of the First Amendment? Who does Leslie Chesterfield actually think she is?

Maybe the Chesterfield agency isn't really a modeling agency at all. I mean, think about it. The CIA stands for the Central Intelligence Agency. The full name of Leslie's company is the Chesterfield International Modeling Agency. The *CIMA*. CIA. CIMA.

Coincidence? I don't think so.

Busy Bee

No lie. The new schedule that Leslie had me on kicked my butt. Don't even get me started on my trainer, Jenisa. She is like five feet two inches of pure muscle, and even at six in the morning, she's wide awake and cheerful. I don't know what made me more nauseous, having to do thirty pop-ups in a row (dropping into push-up position, then jumping straight up into standing) or the fact that Jenisa always wanted to have philosophical discussions about the meaning of life before the crack of dawn.

Tuesdays and Thursdays were jam-packed with classes, then on Mondays, Wednesdays, and Fridays, I had to take my portfolio around to potential clients on "go sees" all day. Then after a whole day of hearing, "Too tall/too short/too thin to be a plus/too big to be a plus," I had to rush back to school for my 6 P.M. History of Western Music. Sometimes, in the middle of the professor playing a baroque chamber orchestra, I took a little nap. Luckily, it was a big class and

I don't snore. Well, if I do, nobody's ever told me.

It kinda sucked not being able to tutor Kevin anymore. We met at Starbucks for our last session, but instead of being Minnie the Moocher, I actually treated for the caramel macchiato and a double-chocolate-chip Frappuccino for him.

"So Kevin, I can't tutor you anymore," I told him, setting the beverages down on the little table between us.

"What's the deal?" he asked. "I got a B on my last exam. With your help, I'm tearing up this math thing."

I could see that a B meant a lot to him. Considering the D he'd been at when we started, I had to agree.

"It's just that I've got this other job," I said.

I don't know why I didn't just come out and tell him. I guess it was because I knew that I was already twenty pounds more than when I met him. I didn't want him to burst out laughing when I said that I was a model. But he kept pressing.

"What kind of job?" he said. "You've got other students you like better than me?"

Honestly, besides Chela and, of course, Brian, there was no one I really hung out with other than Kevin. So I decided to fess up.

"I'm doing some modeling," I said.

"That's kinda fresh," he said, flashing me one of his butter-melting grins. "I always thought you were a dime piece."

"A dime piece?" I asked. Being from Philly, I knew a

lot of hip-hop lingo, but Kevin was always one step ahead of me.

"You know, a perfect ten," he said. "A dime piece."

My whole face went red. Kevin was just trying to make me feel better. Was it national Be Nice to a Chubby Girl Day? I knew Kevin was bad at math, but I didn't know just how bad until that moment. I was a ten plus four: a perfect size fourteen, maybe.

"Whatever," I said. "You know, it's not real modeling; it's plus-size modeling."

Kevin put down his drink and looked really bothered.

"Bee, I've been in show business for a little bit longer than you, so let me tell you now," he said. "There's a lot of people in this industry that are going to try to pull you down just because they think you're trying to steal their shine. You're never going to succeed unless you believe you deserve everything you've got."

"Okay," I said, opening his textbook and trying to change the subject. "Now, let's talk about polynomials."

But he closed the book and said, "I'll get another tutor. Let's just talk. You're coming to my record-release party on Thursday night, right?"

"Oh yeah, definitely," I said uncertainly.

"And if you can't come, then call me," he said. "This is a VIP pass, so you'll go straight to the front of the line."

"Really?" I said, which is what I always say when I can't quite believe something and which my mother calls the painful elaboration of the obvious.

I looked at the invite. The party was at Bungalow 8. Chela and I tried to get into that club once, and we stood outside for two hours before we gave up. And believe me, that's saying something. Chela has never met a bouncer she couldn't charm.

"Bungalow 8. So many people will be there, you won't even notice," I said, slipping the invite into my fake Louis Vuitton.

"I'd notice," he said.

"Oh yeah?" I asked coyly.

"I notice *everything*," he said, raising an eyebrow.

Then he left. And I sat there in Starbucks, for a long time, staring into my four-dollar beverage.

What did Kevin mean when he said he noticed *everything*? Maybe he meant it when he said I was a dime piece. Did he really care if I came to his launch party? And if he didn't care, why did he give me a VIP pass? This may seem like the painful elaboration of the obvious, but I'm just going to go ahead and say it: Boys are confusing. After a while, I realized it didn't matter what Kevin wanted. I wanted Brian, and that was all the confusing boy drama I could handle.

By the time I got home, I'd talked myself out of going to the party. One, I was in love with Brian, and as soon as he learned that I was a model, he was going to figure out what a dime piece I really was. Two, Kevin was a rapper and was probably going to end up dating some kind of video vixen.

On Wednesday, I got booked for a Thursday shoot. Which meant I'd have to miss Kevin's party anyway. Which was partly a relief and partly sucked because it was probably my one and only chance to get into Bungalow 8. I gave my VIP pass to Chela under the express condition that she find Kevin and explain to him that I had to work. She promised. That is, she promised after she jumped up and down and screamed, "Get out! A VIP pass to Bungalow 8? Get out!" about a dozen times.

My shoot on Thursday was for *Lad*, a British men's magazine. The concept for the shoot was that I was supposed to be some sort of sexy farmhand. The location was a real farm in upstate New York. They sent a car service to pick me up, but still it was a haul. It was a two-hour drive up there and a two-hour drive back. The photographer wanted to shoot at the magic hour, right before sunset, which meant I wasn't going to get back until really late.

My call time was two P.M., and when I showed up, there wasn't a single person I knew. The photographer, Laurence Goodman, was a big bruiser of a guy who looked more like a football player than a fashion photographer. He was also a mind reader because five seconds after shaking my hand, he pointed to his knee and said, "Bum knee. Ruined my chances at pro ball. My best friend plays for the Giants, but I get to hang out with a lot of pretty girls."

Then he introduced me to the whole crew: Rosie, the stylist; Teresa, the makeup artist; and Sonia, who did hair.

I almost fell over when I saw the wardrobe: supertight Daisy Duke shorts, brightly colored gingham blouses, and super-high Candie's wedges.

"I don't know if I can fit in that stuff," I said nervously. Leslie had me meeting with a nutritionist once a week, and I was on this Zone meal-delivery service. But Chela and I had gone out for burgers and fries the weekend before, and I was already feeling a good two pounds heavier.

"Don't worry about it," Rosie said. "I pulled a bunch of sizes, and you're going to look supercute." She gave me a sympathetic smile. Cute, maybe. But I'd be freezing. It was already late November, and we were shooting a feature for the June issue.

Laurence and his assistants had prepared three setups: one with me milking a cow, one of me grooming a horse, and the third of me wearing galoshes and throwing handfuls of corn at a pen of pigs.

Did I mention that I grew up in Philadelphia and live in New York City? That in my world, milk came from cows, horses were for driving carriages around Central Park, and don't get me started on pigs. Ever since I read *Charlotte's Web* in third grade, I tried really, really hard not to think about where bacon came from.

I went into hair and makeup, and I have to admit they did an amazing job. Sonia sewed all these hair extensions into my own hair giving me these long ringlet curls like a Botticelli goddess.

I was admiring myself in the mirror, something that I do, like, never, when it occurred to me that maybe I could make Kevin's record-release party. I'd call him as soon as the shoot wrapped and see if he could leave me an extra ticket at the door. After all, it would be a shame not to go out when I had all this fake, fabulous hair and diva makeup on.

Laurence led me over to the cow, which was WAY bigger up close than it had looked from the other side of the barn, where they'd set up hair, makeup, and wardrobe.

"Okay, Bee, the first thing we want you to do is milk this cow," Laurence said.

"You mean, pretend to milk the cow," I said. I put my hand on the udder, and it was not a nice feeling. I shivered. I knew my day rate was seven a day, which was ridiculously high. But today I was really, really earning it.

Laurence seemed to feel my pain. "Do whatever makes you comfortable," he said.

I pretended to milk the cow and tried to remember all the things that Leslie had told me. Connect to the camera with my eyes. Smile, but not so wide that you could see halfway down my throat. I threw my weave around and even wiggled my hips in my Daisy Dukes. It was fun. It felt like I was finally a real model.

Laurence seemed really happy too. He kept jumping all

around, catching me from different angles. "That's great, Bee," he said. "More like that. Not too sexy, we're going for all-American-girl sweetness here."

All of a sudden, I felt like someone had thrown scalding-hot water onto my leg. I screamed and slumped onto the floor of the barn. "Ow, ow, ow."

Everyone came rushing over and Laurence, who'd apparently grown up on a farm in Wisconsin, was fighting to hold back a grin.

"It burns," I said, holding on to my leg and rolling around on the floor. "It really, really burns."

"Cow pee usually does," he said, pulling me to my feet. "You'll be okay. Let's take a break, get you a shower and have some dinner."

A cow, an honest-to-goodness cow, used me as her own private urinal. So much for the glamorous life of a fashion model.

By the time I'd showered, had dinner with the crew, and got back into hair, makeup, and wardrobe, it was another two hours. If everything went well, I could be in the car by nine P.M., then at Kevin's party by eleven P.M. A little late, seeing as I had an early morning go see, but I could at least go in for a hot minute to say hello and congrats.

In the next setup, I was grooming a horse. I wore another pair of Daisy Dukes, a white T-shirt, a suede vest, and a pair of cowboy boots.

It was all good. I don't know a lot about horses, but this

one was a beauty: a gorgeous chestnut brown Appaloosa with a patch of white on its haunches.

Then the horse started to poop. I tried not to complain, but the odor got stronger and stronger.

"Oh my God, this horse smells," I said as quietly and professionally as I could.

"I know, darling," Laurence said. "But the manure is not in the photograph, and we'll lose the light if we take the time to muck the stable out."

I tried to give good strong model faces, to contour my body in interesting shapes against the strong profile of the horse. But after about twenty minutes, I just gave up.

"I can't take the smell," I said. I felt like I was going to pass out.

"Sure, you can," Laurence said. "You're a pro. Give me some great shots, and we'll move on to the next setup."

I took the brush from Laurence's assistant, then lovingly brushed the horse as if his poop didn't smell to the high heavens. Finally Laurence called, "Okay, next setup."

I was so excited that I threw the brush down, and it hit the horse's foot. The Appaloosa started to kick up manure, and before I knew it, my bare legs were covered with the stuff.

"No, no, no," I said, staggering away. "This can't be happening to me."

Laurence called out to Rosie, the stylist, "Another shower for Miss Bee and make it snappy because I'd like a nice twilight for the final shot."

I showered, got dressed again, and the hair and make-up people dolled me up with a new look. Laurence led me over to the pigpen and gave me a feed bag full of corn. I was wearing a 1950s-style housedress, pumps, and my hair had been teased into a giant bouffant.

"This one's easy," Laurence said. "You'll stand on this side of the fence, and all you have to do is toss corn at the pigs. Toss it far and they won't be anywhere near you."

"Got it," I said. "Then we're out of here, right?"

"You'll be off faster than a pack of dogs on a three-legged cat," Laurence said, flashing me a huge smile.

It had been a crappy day, literally and figuratively, and Laurence had kept the mood on the set light.

"Okay, Bee," he said. "I'm coming in for a close-up."

"No problem," I said, smiling sweetly.

"I'd like to get a little closer," Laurence said, inching in. "Could you arch your back? A little more, a little more? Like a ballet dancer. Did you ever dance ballet?"

The answer to that question is no, I never danced ballet. Which is probably why I ended up toppling over the pigpen fence and plopping right into the mud. And because I was holding a sack of corn feed, I was surrounded by pigs eager to eat the treats that had also fallen in the mud.

Maybe it was because it was so late or maybe it was because I really did look ridiculous, but everyone just burst out laughing. After a while, I started laughing too. Everything that could've gone wrong had gone wrong, but I'd survived and it was over.

By the time we'd wrapped, it was nine P.M., and by the time the car dropped me off, it was almost 11 P.M. I thought about going to the party, but one, I was exhausted; two, I couldn't face the crowds; and three, I wasn't entirely sure I didn't smell ever so slightly of cow pee and horse manure.

I took my fourth shower of the day and crawled into bed to watch the news. When I was still dating Brian, I only watched CNN. But ever since he'd broken up with me, I'd gone back to my old favorite, *MTV News*.

I was lying in the bed all warm and toasty in my *Bewitched* flannel pajamas when I saw that the anchor was flashing my picture on the screen. It was of me in Italy and I was on the speedboat with Lucho "Touch Me Anywhere" Abruzzi.

"The fashion industry is abuzz with talk of a hot young model that they are calling the new Savannah Hughes. Her name is Bee Wilson, and she's featured in Prada's new resort-wear campaign."

Oh. My. *God*.

Then the anchor cut to an interview with Savannah Hughes, walking the red carpet at a movie premiere earlier that evening.

"So Savannah," the reporter said, "what do you make of this girl they are calling the new Savannah Hughes?"

Her date was some sort of indie-rock singer and she

held on to his arm like they were madly in love. "Well, that's ridiculous," she said, beaming the happy smile of a woman who's never known what it's like to be covered in burning cow pee. "In order for there to be the next Savannah Hughes, the original would have to give up the throne. And as you can see, darling, I'm here and I'm fabulous."

It was more than a little weird to see myself on TV and to hear Savannah Hughes talk about me as if I were competition. Well, that was the definition of life on planet Strange. But Savannah had echoed my own thoughts. "That's ridiculous," I said out loud, and turned off the TV. I was so tired that I quickly fell asleep.

About two hours later, I got a call from Chela. "Yo, turn on your TV," she said. Her voice sounded extra loud, like she was talking through a megaphone.

"Too sleepy," I whispered into the phone. You know how sometimes when you wake up in the middle of a dream, you think if you don't talk or if you talk really quietly, you can get right back to sleep? That was my plan, but it wasn't happening. Chela was too amped.

"You're on *MTV News*! And Savannah Hughes is popping all kinds of mess," she said.

"I saw it," I said. "They aired it earlier in the evening. How was the party?"

"It was incredible," she said.

"Did you give Kevin my message?"

"Man, I couldn't get near him," Chela said. "He was absolutely swamped. It was like he was Lupe Fiasco, Kanye West, and Common all rolled into one. But I gave the message to one of his managers."

"Okay," I said.

"Bee, you're a star, *mami*," Chela said. "How can you sleep at a time like this?"

I guess I slept really well because when I woke up the next morning, the phone was off the hook and I had no recollection of telling Chela good-bye.

Bee Season

They say there's no such thing as bad publicity, and
Savannah dissing me on MTV turned out to be the biggest
boost to my career. Leslie got all these calls from people
wanting to meet "the next Savannah Hughes," and I started booking jobs left and right: a Lane Bryant jeans commercial, an ad for Swatch, a catalog shoot for H&M. It was
amazing to feel so in demand. The more I worked, the better my modeling got. Tyra Banks once said that a true supe
has more than 275 smiles at her disposal. I was nowhere
near that good. But as I practiced in the mirror, I realized
I had twenty or thirty camera-ready "looks," and the photographers were more and more pleased with my work.

A few weeks later, we got the break that Leslie had
been hoping for all along: a national campaign for lingerie
with billboards in twenty-six cities. It was an ad for Trophy
Life, the hip-hop clothing line, and the advertising agency
had come up with the idea of casting six plus-size models,
all of different races, in a series of ads that read, "I love

my Trophy Life." They were even going to shoot a television commercial, a kind of "behind the scenes," at the photo shoot. I'd gotten used to the chaos of a still photo shoot. But I'd never done TV before. Did I really want to be shaking my moneymaker on national TV?

Chela said, "Come on, Bee. This isn't about you. It's about girls seeing healthy-size women looking beautiful."

I said, "So 'healthy' is the new euphemism for 'fat'?"

She sighed. "You are not fat. Just relax and be yourself. Do—"

"I know, I know," I said. "Do *you*. I mean, do *me*."

* * *

Leslie made sure that I had Andy doing my hair and Syreeta doing my makeup at the Trophy Life shoot so I would feel completely comfortable. I walked into this gigantic studio at Chelsea Piers, and it was like a party had started the night before and never ended. It was seven-thirty A.M., but there was a DJ booth set up and this cool-looking girl with a 'fro-that-would-not-quit was spinning tunes. There was a section with film cameras. There were scrims and lights set up for the still photo shoot. And most of all, there were racks and racks of clothes.

Five models had been booked for the shoot, and, of course, we were all getting ready in one room. I was the first to arrive. After my wake-up-call fiasco in Italy, Leslie had drilled it through my head that models have a bad reputation for always being late and that one way to stand out was to be early. "Take your homework with you," she said. So I made it a point to show up at least an hour before call time. I set myself up at a makeup table near the window and was working on some physics equations when this girl shoved me. It took me a second to realize who she was: Savannah Hughes.

"You're in my spot," she said.

I was too stunned to respond—I was having a hard time registering that, in fact, Savannah Hughes was talking to me. Well, yelling.

"Are you deaf?" she said. "Move."

Then she shoved me.

I was sure that this couldn't be happening with two dozen people running around. But that was the thing, it was early, everyone was prepping, no one was paying attention to the models yet.

I don't know what gave me the courage to stand up to her or, rather, sit down to her. But I didn't get up. Maybe I was just too terrified to move. She rolled her eyes at me, issued an additional warning—"You better watch your back, bitch"—and walked away.

I couldn't believe someone like that would even care about someone as unimportant as me. Savannah was a supermodel. When I was in junior high, she was on the cover of *Elle Girl* and *Seventeen* constantly. She dated rock stars and was always on TV, walking the red carpet. Then she had a nervous breakdown and admitted that she had an eating disorder. After her treatment, she gained forty pounds (she'd weighed about ten pounds before) and reinvented herself as a "plus" model.

When Andy showed up and started to work on my hair, he told me the whole story. "Just look at her; she hates herself," he whispered to me. "She's not really big enough to be a plus model, and she's too big to compete with the skinny girls. I heard her tell her makeup artist that this was the last 'fat-girl' shoot she was going to do, that she's heard of this new diet pill that's supposed to be amazing, and she's going to 'lose the weight once and for all.'"

This just goes to show you how I'm a product of my society because, despite the fact that I was now making ten thousand dollars a day as a plus-size model, the only thing I really heard was "new diet pill that's supposed to be amazing."

The photographer came over and told us we were going to do two different looks that morning. In one, we'd all be wearing white camisoles and lacy boy shorts. This was for the black-and-white campaign. In the second one, we'd wear color, and he'd shoot us lying down in a pile of rose petals.

As we dressed for the black-and-white shoot, I met the other girls. Elsie was like this classic, blonde-haired, blue-eyed girl. But the minute she opened her mouth, it was like she was some whiz-kid investment banker.

"Sell, no, don't sell," she said. "Why do I have a broker if you aren't going to tell me what you think?"

Then she hung up her cell phone in a huge huff. Listening to her talk, I thought about the savings I had in the bank, earning 3 percent in my savings account. I was going to ask her for some investment tips when she spoke to me.

"If the Federal Reserve doesn't lower interest rates, the market's going to collapse," she said when I passed her on my way to wardrobe.

"What?" I asked, confused.

Melody, one of the other girls, just laughed. "She's not talking to you. She's listening to Bloomberg Radio on her iPod."

Melody was African American, from California, a complete yoga girl. She was dressed first and had brought along a mat that she laid out in a corner, off to the side. It was amazing the positions she could put her body into. "Yoga helps to center me in the midst of all this madness," she said, and everything about her seemed so serene and lovely. Memo to self: Yoga makes you not only bendy, but pretty.

Prageeta was Indian and seemed to be surgically attached to her BlackBerry. Andy told me that Prageeta had a much older boyfriend, this novelist who was really famous, though I'd never heard of him.

Once we were dressed, Syreeta and all the other makeup artists put all kinds of makeup on our legs and stomachs. "Contour lines," Syreeta explained. "To give you a little definition." It was weird, and not for nothing, it tickled. I was doing my best not to laugh, but as I looked around,

I could see the other girls were struggling too. I caught Elsie's eye and made a face like my physics professor. She burst out laughing, and soon we were all doubled over. Everyone except for Savannah, of course. Terry, the photographer, came running over and said, "Whatever the joke is, save it! I need this energy for the shoot."

They rushed us through makeup, and he began to take our picture. It's strange to model with a group of girls that you've never met before. The idea was to look like we were all old friends, but in reality, it felt kind of fake and awkward. Savannah was the fakest of them all. The minute Terry started shooting, it was like someone had flipped a switch in her. She came alive. The minute Terry put the camera down, she turned cold as ice. It was like that all day. We all got closer and more comfortable, sharing stories about guys and food and clothes: when they let you keep the clothes, when they don't, what the protocol was. But Savannah made sure we knew that she breathed a higher plane of air. Once the group shot was over, she got on the phone with her agent and screamed, "This is it. I can't do any more of these jobs. These fat girls disgust me."

The words just hung in the air, and it seemed, for a moment, that we were all frozen in time as well. Melody was in downward dog. Prageeta was texting her boyfriend. Elsie and I were buying some boots, at the wholesale price, from the stylists. We all heard her. None of us moved. Then Andy said in this super-loud voice, "Bitch, please." And the tension was broken, the cord that had been pulled so tightly all day just snapped.

We all got dressed for our individual shots, and I was really nervous. I tended to do well with someone else in the picture, if I had someone to play off of, or, to be honest, someone to copy a little bit. But when it was me, all by myself, I still felt really intimidated.

It didn't help that I was in a leopard-print baby doll that reminded me of the outfit that I'd worn when I tried, very unsuccessfully, to seduce Brian. From the moment I put it on, I had this flashback of bad memories. I felt viscerally sick to my stomach for a minute.

Melody could tell that I was nervous, and she came over to me and whispered in my ear, "Just tune all of these other jokers out. Think about someone you love." Which, of course, made me think of Brian again and made me feel even worse.

When I walked onto the set, which the production people had covered in all of these funky jungle prints, Terry came over to talk to me.

"I understand you're nervous," he said. "It's always hard to be sexy when a dozen people are watching."

Sure, that was definitely a factor. But it's also hard to be sexy when you've never actually had sex. Of course, I couldn't tell him that.

"Just pretend that no one else is here and give me all you've got," Terry said, walking off the set. "Remember, I need you to own it. Make me believe that any guy in the world would be lucky to get a sneak peek of you in your Trophy Life lingerie."

One of Terry's assistants started playing music, and I was kind of in shock. It was Kevin's new single, "He's Not the One." Listening to him rap reminded me of how easy it was to hang out with him, and I started dancing around and getting into a groove.

"Okay, Bee," Terry said. "That's nice, you're loosening up, but I need you to engage with the camera. Really show me you've got what it takes to be a supe."

I started posing, moving just my torso, turning my head ever so slightly, all the things that I'd been practicing in the Lotte Berk dance class that Leslie made me take on Saturday afternoons.

Then I threw both hands up in the air, like a *V* for Victory sign, and out of nowhere, Savannah started screaming, "That's my signature move! She's copied everything from me, and I've worked too hard to let her—"

Before anyone could stop her, she was on the set and she'd wrestled me to the floor. Skinny or plus, she was one strong girl.

I was trying to push her off of me when I felt the snip. She was holding a pair of scissors, and she'd cut a huge chunk of my hair.

She held it up and waved it around. "Now let's see what the bald bitch can do."

Terry said, "Savannah, you're dismissed from the set. Get her out of here."

Andy, Syreeta, and all the crew members were gathered around me. Terry asked me if I was all right. And I was all right. But I couldn't stop crying.

Syreeta said, "Girl, do you want to see a mirror?"

I nodded. But when she brought it over, I just started to bawl even louder. I looked like a crazy person. She'd managed to snip six inches off the left side of my head.

Terry said, "What do you think, Andy? How do we fix it?"

I looked up at Andy, hopeful that he could give me some kind of miracle. Without my hair, and having all this extra weight, I looked like a pumpkin.

He knelt down next to me and ran his hands through my hair.

"I could give her a weave," he said, speaking not to me, but to Terry. "But actually, I think we should cut it, give her a razor-cut bob, shorter in the back, longer in the front, with bangs. And we should dye it red. It'll be fierce."

Terry said, "Okay, let's do it."

Four hours later, I had a whole new haircut. Andy had to put in a few tracks of weave on the left side, and I cried the whole time. But by the time he was done, I felt like a new person. My hair was fire-engine red, like the girl in *Run Lola Run*. It had all these jagged edges, and it felt really light, not thick and wavy the way it had all my life.

All of a sudden, when I went back to the set in the leopard babydoll, I didn't feel like Bee who'd been rejected by her college sweetheart. Or premed Bee who was taking eighteen credits because she was such an overachiever. I felt like model Bee, who was a little bit bad and a whole lot of fun.

"Perfect," Terry said as he clicked away. "This is what I've been wanting to see from you all day. Give me a little more rock 'n' roll. You're onstage now, and there's a stadium full of people who are screaming out your name."

I kept mugging for the camera, and while before I was doing little turns here and there, all of a sudden I wasn't afraid to use my whole body.

When we were all done, Terry said, "Honestly, Bee, I don't think there was a single picture in this evening's roll that wasn't billboard worthy. Good job."

Back in the dressing room, Syreeta helped me take off my makeup, and Andy smoothed out my hair with a flat-iron so that the cut would last for a few more days.

"Mark my words," Andy said, "this is going to change your career as a model. You were cute before. But you're stunning now."

"And all because Savannah Hughes went crazy and attacked me with a pair of scissors!" I laughed. "Who would believe it?"

"God works in mysterious ways," Andy said. "You may have to send that *biatch* flowers."

Bee Joins the A-List

To celebrate both the Trophy Life campaign and my making the Dean's List, Leslie called to invite me to lunch at Aquavit. I jumped into the shower and tried to decide what to wear. Leslie was more than the head of the modeling agency; she was like the cool girl you always wanted to be. I didn't want to look overly made up, but I wanted, at least for tonight, to look like a model. So I threw on this lavender Versace top that a stylist had given me on a shoot, with a pair of wide-legged khakis and a little khaki jacket.

I went downstairs, where Leslie was waiting in her "car." By car, she meant a town car, with a driver, which I discovered is how rich people get around New York. All those limos you see going back and forth? Out of towners and teenagers going to the prom.

"You look really nice," Leslie said.

"Thanks," I said, grateful that I'd chosen my outfit carefully. I'd never been the über-fashionable type, but I was beginning to pick up a few tips from my photo shoots.

And more and more, designers and stylists sent me cool clothes as gifts.

Once we settled into a primo booth at the restaurant, Leslie said, "So I have to tell you, there's been some fallout from the shoot."

"Do you mean my hair?" I asked.

"No, your hair is fantastic," she said. "What a lucky accident. Clients are loving it, and we're going to have to update your portfolio with a whole new shoot."

But I knew Leslie well enough to know that she didn't dole out praise easily. Something bad had happened. I'd done something or said something to offend a client or a photographer. It was five minutes to midnight and I was Cinderella, about to be transformed back into rags.

"As you know, Savannah Hughes was cut out of the Trophy Life campaign," Leslie said. "The client felt she was too thin to portray the plus ideal."

Great, now I'd have to watch my back for psycho models wielding scissors wherever I went.

"Savannah seemed to take an instant dislike to me," I said.

Leslie nodded. "You know, this kind of thing happens all the time, Bee. You're the new girl on the block, and the buzz on you is big. Savannah got cut out of the campaign, and instead of dealing with her own yo-yo dieting issues and the fact that her agent can't get her bookings because no one knows what size she'll be when she shows up, she's focused on you as her enemy. Just watch your back."

Great. Like I needed one more thing to think about.

Leslie said, "Okay, enough about her."

She gestured to the waiter and ordered two glasses of champagne. When he brought them over, a huge smile spread across Leslie's face. She said, "Bee, you've really knocked it out of the park. Your grades are up. You've got a national ad campaign. We're getting more and more calls about you every day."

She lifted a glass of champagne and said, "To you, Bee."

She pulled out the June issue of *Glamour* magazine and there I was, with all the other girls, in a two-page spread. "We love our Trophy Life," the ad said.

I took the magazine from her and just stared at it for a while. It was strange to see myself, parts of myself that no one ever saw—especially my stomach and my hips and my thighs—in a magazine. There was no doubt about it. I wasn't like Savannah—I was 100 percent plus. The question is, did I really love my curves? Would Brian find them so winning? And why did those questions feel like one and the same to me?

* * *

When I got home that night, Chela called me on my cell.

"What are you doing, Bee?"

"Just prepping for finals."

"Have you seen the Trophy Life ad?"

"I saw *Glamour* today. Leslie took me to Aquavit to celebrate."

"That's all you've seen?"

"Yep. It's kind of cool."

"Well, I'm taking you out to dinner," Chela said. "Can you be ready in an hour?"

"Sure," I said. "I never turn down free food."

* * *

Chela picked me up at my place, and we hopped on the 1 train downtown.

"Where are we going?" I asked.

"Virgil's BBQ," Chela said.

I grimaced. Despite what people thought, being a plus-size model didn't actually mean that I could eat anything I wanted. On the contrary, I had to be super-fit. I worked out with Jenisa, the trainer Leslie had found for me, at this super-snazzy private gym three days a week. And I ate salads six days a week. Sundays were my cheat days, but this wasn't a Sunday.

Chela said, "Why the face?"

"I can't have barbecue. I've got a big shoot on Monday. I've got to be good and eat something bunny worthy."

"Okay, how about we go to Zen Palate?"

Zen Palate is an Asian vegetarian restaurant. It'd super-hard to pig out there.

"Thanks, Chela."

"No problem, girlfriend. I'm all about supporting a sista

in her quest to be healthy. I just need to stop at the Virgin megastore to pick up a DVD for my fella."

We hopped off the train at Times Square. I started walking toward the Virgin megastore, but when we got to Forty-third Street, Chela stopped and pointed up.

There I was, all by myself, in a black-and-white shot, wearing nothing but my undies, on a giant billboard hanging over Times Square.

All of a sudden I blurted out, "I can't wait until Brian sees this!"

Chela looked surprised. "Why do you care what that loser thinks?"

"I don't," I said, covering. "I just want him to see the billboard so he can know HOW big a loser he really is."

This, as you have probably realized, was a lie. I'd been trying to get some props for my modeling from Brian for a while now. I still didn't have Brian back. I'd taken my portfolio to a Blue Key meeting one afternoon to show him what I was up to, and he just totally blew me off.

"Modeling?" he had said. "Do you honestly think that with all the problems there are in the world, I'm interested in something as superficial as modeling photos?"

I didn't point out that his bathroom walls were plastered with *Sports Illustrated* swimsuit photos. I just skulked away. But I couldn't help but hang on to the thing that Chela had said when we'd first met about Brian being a boomerang. I wanted him to come back to me. He just needed to see the new me. I mean, really see.

Ever since Leslie Chesterfield had offered me my first modeling gig, life had been like a fairy tale. Sure, I had some rough patches. Savannah Hughes had decided that she was my evil stepsister and evil stepmother all wrapped up into one, and I had to work my ample-size booty off to squeak out a B+ in advanced physics, but honestly, what more could a girl want? I was a model. I was premed at a top school. I had an awesome best friend. All I needed to complete the picture was a boyfriend, and the only boyfriend I wanted was Brian. I mean, he'd been building homes for Habitat for Humanity since he was in high school; he'd helped to build *thirty* homes for poor families. He'd gone to India after the tsunami. He read six newspapers a day, and he was probably going to be president of the United States one day. I mean, really. There was a seat on Air Force One with my name on it.

14

Like Bee to Honey

Everyone was talking about the Trophy Life ads. They launched a Website featuring us, the Trophy Life girls—and Leslie told me that my picture was getting a million hits a day. I tried to read all of the posts, but it was bizarre, like reading about a total stranger:

"Bee. It's such a relief to turn on the TV and see a 'real woman' like you, instead of a stick figure. Thank you for all you do."

"A few weeks ago, I went out to dinner with some girls from my school, and I just felt so full. I'd totally stuffed my face. So this one girl showed me how to make myself throw up, and I just felt much better. Like I wasn't such a pig. I was going to try it again when I saw you in a magazine, and I thought, I bet that girl never makes herself throw up. All of a sudden, it felt disgusting to me."

"I just wish the designers would get a clue. We don't all look like Kate Moss. They need to cater to the larger women's needs."

"I'm a sixteen-year-old high school junior, and after I read that Bee was not only a model, but a premed student at Columbia University, I decided that's where I want to apply. I got the application today. Thank you, Bee."

Letters like the last one were my favorite. But on the Website, there were literally thousands of posts. I could read all day long and never get through them all. Leslie said that the agency was getting a sack full of letters every day and that she had one assistant whose entire job it was to stamp my autograph on pictures and send them out. If that's not the definition of weirdness, then I don't know what is.

I was getting more and more calls for bookings, though I couldn't work as much as Leslie wanted me to. I was determined not to let it affect my schoolwork, so I turned down a lot of bookings—even though my day rate had doubled since the billboard in Times Square. There just weren't enough hours in a day to do everything!

❊ ❊ ❊

That weekend, after my last class on Thursday, I jumped into a cab to La Guardia Airport. I had a flight to Miami. I was doing a swimsuit shoot for a German magazine. I know you're thinking, what's the big deal? I was already rocking my skivvies on a billboard in Times Square. But the whole Trophy Life photo shoot felt more like a campaign for self-esteem than about showing off all my private parts. The swimsuit campaign was different, and I didn't understand why they had booked me.

* * *

The Friday night before, I was over at Leslie's for taco night. Of course, at Leslie's that meant ground-turkey tacos on baked tortillas, but it was still pretty yum. She'd practically adopted me as her little sister. Well, her younger sister who was taller and heavier than she was. Dinner was over, and Leslie's husband was off to meet his friends at some snazzy cigar bar. I'd just read *The Day I Swapped My Dad for Two Goldfish* to Leslie's son Jackson. He was three and the definition of adorable. Reading him a bedtime story on a Friday night was easily the highlight of my week.

Leslie and I were eating the tiniest bowls of blood orange gelato and listening to the old CD from Air in her "media" room. It probably goes without saying that Les's media room was the size of my entire apartment. Everything in the media room responded to Leslie's voice, so if she said, "Air. *Talkie-Walkie.* Track six," that's what would come wafting through the speakers that were so high tech, you didn't even see them; they were built into the walls and the bookcases and even the huge leather club chairs.

"Even the girls who do plus-size suits have flat stomachs," I whined to Leslie. "Why do they even want me?"

"The Germans like big girls," she said. "Think about it this way. It's colder than a witch's tit in New York. You're getting an all-expenses-paid weekend to Miami."

"I know, I know."

"They've booked Andy and Syreeta for hair and make-up."

"That's cool."

"It'll be great," Leslie said reassuringly. Then, changing subjects, she said, "I wish I were Charlotte Gainsbourg."

My mouth nearly dropped on the floor. In all honesty, a little gelato drooled out of the side of my mouth. Leslie was blonde, gorgeous, successful, happily married, and loaded. People like her don't dream about being somebody else. Which is what I told her.

"Oh, there's a part of me that would love to be tall and French with brown hair and a sexy accent. Everybody dreams about being somebody else," Leslie said. "It's the way we're built."

* * *

In Miami, I stayed at the Delano, which is the definition of hotness. From the moment the porters open the big glass doors, you feel like you're walking into a movie. There are thin white curtains that blow in the wind, and there's a long lobby that leads right out to the beach. Nearly everything is white: white couches, white lamps, white candles, and dark-wood floors. I saw Syreeta checking in, and we had dinner by the pool. I was really good and had a calamari salad and a virgin mojito. Truth be told, I never used to like salads. But the more I traveled for photo shoots, the more I realized that the wilting lettuce and tasteless toma-toes my mom used to serve with Thousand Island dressing could hardly be considered a salad. The calamari salad had all kinds of lettuces, hearts of palm, sweet bananas, and a sesame orange dressing. I was going to have a big fat chocolaty dessert, but Syreeta reminded me that it was my first swimsuit. I'd hate to add overnight sugar bloat to my list of insecurities, so we split a fruit plate instead.

The next morning, it was a six A.M. call at the beach. I actually liked getting up so early by this point in my modeling career. My room had an ocean view, and I slept with my windows open, even though Leslie tells me that I've got to be more careful in hotels. I fell asleep to the sounds of the waves crashing and woke up the same way.

I was worried that I would look like a sausage squeezed into all the tiny swimsuits. But they fit fine. I told Syreeta how surprised I was that I felt comfortable in the suits.

"Aren't you glad you skipped dessert last night?"

What I said was, "Yes, you're totally right." But I hadn't stopped thinking about the "chocolate bomb" on the menu and fully intended to have it tonight. I guess I must've been drooling or something 'cause Syreeta said, "You're thinking about that cake, aren't you?"

"Oh yeah," I said, grinning devilishly. "I thought being a plus-size model meant that I could eat whatever I wanted."

Syreeta shook her head. "All things in moderation. Being a plus-size model means that you *can* eat. Those other girls don't get to eat at all."

I thought about this for a second. "Split the chocolate cake with me tonight?"

Syreeta smiled. "It's a deal."

I felt a little exposed, posing on the beach all day as people walked back and forth. When we shot Trophy Life, it had been inside and there were all those other girls with me. But the photographer, Masako, let me play DJ, and I started to rock out to all the music on my iPod. Two tracks into my Shakira mix, I was dancing around and having a great time. And the funny thing was, the more I moved, the more people stopped—men and women—to cheer me on:

"*Wepa, mami!*"

"You are beautiful, girl!"

"*Te quiero, morena.*"

It was snowing in New York, and I was getting paid to shake my groove thing on a beach in Miami. Once and for all, it had been established: It does not suck to be me.

Not everybody was in "you go, girl" mode about the ubiquity of the Trophy Life campaign. The Monday after I got back to New York, this Los Angeles newspaper columnist, Ryan Reynolds, wrote an editorial that ended up making national news. He said, "Every morning, in order to come to work, I'm forced to drive by a giant billboard of five hippo-butt girls declaring that their curves are so winning. But winning to whom? Trophy Life is the name of the underwear these bovine beauties are wearing. They're happy with their cottage cheese asses, so I should be too?

For the record, I'm not. If I want to see out-of-shape girls, with their stomachs spilling over their thongs, then I can stand in line at the all-you-can-eat buffet at my local steak house. The idea that we're supposed to herald overweight women as real-life beauties is the worse kind of feminist tripe."

❊ ❊ ❊

He didn't call any of us by name. He didn't say, "Bee Wilson's cellulite is a personal offense." But it still hurt. For days, I kept walking around and hearing the phrases over and over again, "bovine beauties," "hippo butt."

We were dissed publicly; sliced, diced, and flambéed. Then the countermovement happened. I got flowers from Christy Turlington, the most ginormous arrangement of hydrangeas and roses and lilies I have ever seen in my life. The note said, "I want my daughter to be like you, Bee." It turns out all the girls got them.

2 Cool 2 Bee Forgotten

The president of Trophy Life had this party in our honor at a loft downtown. They even sent a limo to pick us up, and when we got to the party, there was an honest-to-goodness red carpet.

"Damn," Melody said. "I've never walked the red carpet before."

"Come on, we're models," Elsie said. "The one thing we know how to do is walk."

So we did this silly sports-team cheer inside the limo and then sashayed our way down the red carpet like it was something we did every day. The strangest thing is that the photographers knew all of our names. They kept calling out stuff like, "Melody, let me see you smile, baby." And, "Over here, honey Bee."

Inside, there were life-size portraits of us everywhere. We had to give interviews to all the local news stations, and we all kept saying the same thing over and over again:

"I'm very proud to represent real women."

"Real women have curves."

"I do love my body!"

We were all standing together in the press area when a reporter from channel five asked us what we thought of Ryan Reynolds's editorial. I looked from girl to girl, and we all had an identical frozen smile plastered on our faces. Which is why we all burst out laughing when Melody, Miss Sweetness and Light of all people, turned to the camera and very innocently said, "I think it's been a very long time since Ryan Reynolds got laid."

Later on at the party, I was talking to a buyer from Neiman's when Kevin approached me. "Excuse me, may I speak to you for a moment?" he said.

OMG, what was he doing here?

"I haven't seen you in forever, Kev. What have you been up to?" I asked. "Still struggling with math for poets?"

"Well," he said, totally humblelike, which was so not him. "Ever since my video hit the number-one spot on *TRL*, the label's been pressuring me to drop out of school. But I won't do it. . . . "

I was confused.

"Wait a second, you have the number-one video on *TRL*? I thought it was some guy named DJ Go Drop Dead."

Kev laughed. "So you still got jokes."

"No, seriously," I said. "I haven't seen it, but I've heard people talk about this DJ Go Drop Something."

"It's DJ *Drop and Roll*," Kevin said. "That's me."

"Wow!" I said, giving him a hug. "Way to blow up. Sorry I've been out of the loop."

"That's cool," he said. "You're blowing up too. See, unlike you, I've keep tabs on my friends. Like this Trophy Life joint. Yo, I really like you in these ads. I like the whole lot of you girls, but you take the cake. That red hair is wild. Who would've thought that Miss Premed had it in her?"

"You'd be surprised," I said.

"A lot of things surprise me," Kevin said. "Like you not coming to my album-release party."

I was shocked. I couldn't believe he noticed. Chela said more than five hundred people had been there.

"I was there," I said, trying to play it off.

"You weren't there," he said. "But nice try."

He took out a Sharpie marker, and I burst out laughing.

"Are you going to give me your autograph, DJ Drop and Roll?"

"No, I changed my number," he said. He wrote his phone number on the palm of my hand.

Then he said, "Give me your phone." So I handed it to him. He programmed his number into my phone.

"Now you have my number in two places. Don't start talking mess about how you lost it."

* * *

When I got home that night, there was a message from Chela. She'd left me a bunch of messages, and with all the

Trophy Life stuff, I just didn't get a chance to return them. I called her back.

"Oh my God," I said. "You missed the BEST party tonight."

"Really," she said. "How could I miss it when I wasn't invited?"

"Well, it was kind of a work thing," I said.

"You're the star of the campaign and you couldn't score one invite for your best friend?" she asked. Her voice was hot, and I could tell she was getting ready to go into angry-Latina mode. I'd seen her whip it out on other people but never on me.

"When Kevin had his record release, he got a VIP invite for you," she said.

"I know, but . . . "

"But what?" she snapped.

I'm not good at making excuses. Really, I'm not. But I didn't see Chela as part of my modeling life. Did she really have the right to blow a gasket?

"Who was the person who convinced you to go into that first audition in the first place?" she said. "Who's never ever been jealous while you make all that money and fly to exotic places while I wait tables for tips so I can pay my tuition and my room and board?"

"You," I whispered.

"I used to feel kind of sorry for you," Chela said. "It was like you had so much beauty, but you didn't even know it.

That's why I kept telling you to 'do you.' But you know what? If I had known that the real you was such an inconsiderate bitch, then I would have kept my mouth shut."

Did she call me a bitch? Was she right? More importantly, how was I going to fix it? I could feel myself shaking, I was so nervous. It was like breaking up with Brian. Chela was dumping me as her best friend.

"Let me make it up to you," I said. "Let's go out to dinner tomorrow night. Asia de Cuba, my treat."

Chela's been talking about going to Asia de Cuba ever since I met her.

There was silence on the phone.

"Okay," she said. "You better make a reservation 'cause I don't want any drama at the door."

A few hours later, Leslie called with more news. The Trophy Life girls—that's what they were calling us—were going to appear on the *Today* show. I called my father to let him know.

"Do you know that one of your billboards is right in front of my office?"

"That must be strange, Dad."

"A little bit. I could've knocked that Ryan Reynolds guy upside the head talking about my little girl that way."

"Don't sweat it, Dad. He's a loser."

"Loser? I just met her."

This, you should know, is one of Dad's favorite jokes.

"Hey, Bee, could you do your old man a favor? A

couple of the women from my office asked me if I could get them autographed pictures of you. I hate to ask . . . . "

"Dad, please! Autographed pictures are easy."

"My little girl is a star. Can you believe it?"

"I know, Dad."

"How's school?"

"I think I'm going to make the Dean's List this semester," I said, fibbing just a little bit. I'd just gotten a C on a pop quiz in physics, but I was going to pull it together.

"Brainy," my dad said, unaware that I'd lied to him for the very first time. "That's my Bee."

Bee Stings Back

The next morning, we were sitting in the green room of the *Today* show — Prageeta, Melody, Elsie, and me.

"My agent told me that he was approached by a record company," Elsie said. "Someone wants to offer us a deal, put us out as the 'Trophy Life girls.'"

Melody said, "I heard the same thing."

"But that doesn't make sense; they haven't even heard us sing," I said.

Melody said, "Like singing has anything to do with getting a record deal."

Prageeta said, "Anyway, right after the show, I'm off to meet Hanif. He won the Booker, so he's flying in from London."

I said, "Booker? I barely know her."

Prageeta said, "What?"

I said, "It's one of my dad's favorite jokes."

Melody said, "That's our Bee, Patron Saint of Cheese."

* * *

Sitting on the *Today*-show stage with the host, Cadence Connelly, I had to resist the urge to wave into the camera, "Hi, Dad! Hi, Zo!" Instead I tried to remember what Leslie had told me. "The segment will be four minutes, tops. Pay attention. Keep a closed-mouth smile on your face; you never know when the camera is on you. Jump right in and say something. There are five of you; think too long, and you won't get a word in edgewise."

The cameraman counted down the seconds from the commercial break, then Cadence introduced our segment. "You can't have missed them. They're on TV, on the radio, in magazines, and on billboards. Five scantily clad plus-size models, all beautiful. They've garnered praise and criticism. Now they're here in the studio with us."

Then she turned to us and said, "I have to tell you, you're some beautiful girls. If you're what plus looks like, then I might just go ahead and have dessert at lunch today."

"We're tall, we're healthy, we're in proportion, yet most fashion magazines won't book us," Melody said.

"Do you consider yourselves role models?" Cadence asked.

"We have to," I said, jumping in. "At my high school, they had to replace the pipes in the girls' bathroom."

"Why is that?" Cadence asked.

"Because so many girls were throwing up. Over time, the acid in the vomit eats away at the pipes."

Cadence said, "Wow. It's a good thing I eat breakfast

early in the morning. That was a little graphic. I have two daughters; how do I raise them to love *their* baby fat?"

"Get them into sports," Elsie said. "I played soccer throughout high school. I knew that I needed to be strong to get that ball across the field. I knew that being a winner meant building my body up, not trying to whittle it down to fit into a pair of size-four jeans."

"The Ryan Reynolds editorial," Cadence said, bringing up the topic I'd hoped she would skip, "did it hurt your feelings?"

"Of course it hurt," Prageeta said. "It always hurts when someone calls you a name."

Melody said, "Didn't hurt my feelings. I'm laughing all the way to the bank."

Cadence smiled. "That's what I say whenever someone writes something mean about me. So what's next for the Trophy Life girls? Is it true that you're cutting an album?"

"Not true," I said at the same time that Melody said, "Absolutely true."

She had musical ambitions, but the rest of us couldn't carry a tune.

Cadence laughed. "I'll take that as a maybe."

Then before you knew it, the interview was done. Cadence shook hands with each of us, and then she was on to the next segment.

* * *

Prageeta jumped in a car to meet her fiancé, who was

flying in from London; Melody had a go see, but then she asked if Elsie and I wanted to meet her afterward for some celebratory shopping and then dinner. Prageeta said she'd join us for dinner. We were so psyched about our first major talk-show appearance that we couldn't wait to hang out and go over everything a million times.

* * *

Melody and Elsie were roommates in a really fancy building right off of Gramercy Park. This was my first time actually seeing it. A doorman had to call up before I could get on the elevator. When I got inside, it was so beautiful, so luxe, it was like the Beyoncé episode of *MTV Cribs*. There was a huge wall of mirrors, and you could see the Hudson River from each and every one. Prageeta was wearing this cool Marc Jacobs dress that had just been on the cover of *Vogue*. I wanted to ask her how she'd gotten it in our size but decided that might be rude. Then she told me, "I have a friend who works in the Jacobs studio. She can always get something done special. I'll introduce you to her."

Elsie came out and looked equally gorgeous in this ivory Stella McCartney flared jacket with a black turtleneck underneath. I know it sounds like I've become a total label whore, but when you work in fashion, you start to notice these things. At any given photo shoot, I might try on thirty different outfits. And when you spend four hours a day in hair and makeup, you read a lot of fashion magazines.

I'd tried to look "downtown" and cute by wearing this Luella Bartley striped jersey top and a Kangol newsboy cap, but now I felt like I should be delivering the paper rather than staying for dinner. "I look a mess," I said apologetically.

"Shut up, you look cute!" Elsie said. "Isn't that Luella for Target?"

Needless to say, this made me feel much better. Not.

I had been expecting salad from a bag and some Brianna's dressing, but Melody and Elsie had actually ordered in from Nobu.

"I didn't know they delivered," I said to Melody in the kitchen as we pulled out plates and forks. Prageeta had stepped away to text her boyfriend, who had literally just won the Pulitzer Prize or something.

Melody shrugged. "Technically, they don't. But you know, where there's a will, there's a way. . . ."

Melody was wearing this awesome Chloe top that I'd been lusting over for weeks.

"That shirt!" I said as we kissed each other hello. "To die."

I know what you're thinking. When did I become downtown model-y girl? When did I become obsessed with clothes and start throwing around phrases like "to die"? Well, it's like this. I imagine, though I don't know for sure, that when you get a bunch of computer programmers together, they start geeking out and talking about codes and systems. It's the same with models. Except we geek out about makeup, perfume, clothes, and shoes.

Elisa was wearing an amazing pair of Christian Louboutin wedges. We all took a moment to admire them.

"It's really about the craftsmanship," Melody said.

"His sense of color is so French, so whimsical," Prageeta said.

"If you're good to your feet, they'll be good to you," I added.

Everybody stopped and stared at me.

"What?" I asked. "That's what my dad always says. He said expensive shoes are worth it because you've got to take care of your feet."

Elsie laughed. "I don't think these bad boys are what your daddy had in mind."

❉ ❉ ❉

Over dinner, we talked about the Trophy Life campaign. Prageeta said, "Every time I see a picture of myself with the slogan 'I love my Trophy Life,' I have to ask myself, is that the truth?"

Elsie jumped in. "I'm proud of my curves. They'll buy me a house in the Hamptons someday."

"We've got to accept that we're different sizes," Melody said. "I mean, look at flowers. What if there were only one kind of flower? Wouldn't it get boring looking at tulips all the time?"

We all rolled our eyes.

"We're also making good money," Elsie said. "If someone offered you a chance to be a size two, but you'd have to return every dime you made modeling, would you do it?"

Prageeta hesitated. "A size two forever?"

"Yes," Elsie said. "A size two forever." We all took a minute to think about it. All of the Trophy Life girls were so gorgeous, but I don't think one of us could say we hadn't had a moment, or two, or three, or ten million, when we wished we were thinner.

Elsie said, "Well, I can tell you right now that I wouldn't do it. Plus is where my business is. I got my mind on my money. And my money on my mind."

Melody turned to me. "What about you, Bee?"

What about me? I'd never been *that* skinny. I had a hundred grand in the bank, I'd gotten a posh trip to Italy, and I was on a billboard in Times Square. Being a plus-size model gave me a life, and one day, going to medical school would give me a life after modeling.

"I'd rather be plus," I said.

But Prageeta wasn't going to let me off the hook so easily.

"So you feel good about being a size fourteen? Don't you ever look at skinny girls and want to be like them?"

"I don't know. I mean, I look at you and I wish I had skin like yours, but I don't. I wish I had naturally blonde hair like Elsie's, but I don't."

"Which brings me back to the flower argument,"

Melody said.

"Being a plus model made me see myself as beautiful for the first time ever. I know it's the cheesy beauty-pageant answer, but I'd love it if girls saw us in ads and thought, I look like that, so I must be beautiful too."

"Don't you ever wish you were a real model?" Prageeta asked.

"A real model?" Elsie said. "I *am* a real model."

"No, you're a model for chubby girls," Prageeta said. "I'm not hating. I'm one too."

"Come on, P," Melody said. She and Prageeta had clearly been down this path before. "Give it a rest. You've got a great life. You're a top model. You've got this super-smart famous fiancé. You're in a major national ad campaign. No one is going to shed any tears for you."

Prageeta put down her chopsticks. We'd pretty much demolished the platter of sashimi from Nobu and had moved on to calamari salads.

"This is the real," she said. "From here to here, I feel gorgeous." She indicated her face. Which was, for the record, stunning. "From the neck down, I feel fat."

That's when Melody just lost it. "You know what, Prageeta? You're not fat. You're, what, five eight? What do you weigh? A buck seventy?"

Prageeta nodded.

"Look at all of us, we wear off-the-rack designer clothes!" Melody said. "Do you want to know what fat is?

Fat is my mom back in Pasadena. She's five-foot nothing and she's pushing three hundred pounds. She's fat. She's people-staring-in-the-grocery-store fat and kids-making-faces-behind-her-back fat. My mom is the eat-in-bed, stains-on-her-sheet, her-sweat-smells-bad kind of fat. She's not even fifty years old, and she's got high blood pressure and hypertension, and she's borderline diabetic. I save half of every dime I make so that I can take care of her when her body gives out on her, which is going to be sooner rather than later. That is what fat is. It's not being gorgeous and getting fussed over and making twenty-five thousand dollars a day."

We were all silent. I thought about how serene and perfect I always thought Melody was, how she carried her yoga mat with her everywhere and wasn't obnoxious about it. It's just that in modeling, there's a lot of waiting around, and in those moments, you could find Melody off in the corner, doing her yoga thing. I had no idea how much she was carrying around inside. Memo to self: Never say, "I feel fat" again in front of Melody.

We were all eating our calamari salads in silence when Elsie reached over and touched Melody's hand. She said, "That's really rough about your mom."

Melody said, "It's okay."

Elsie said, "But I gotta ask you. Is your day rate really twenty-five thousand dollars a day?"

Everyone burst out laughing. And for the rest of the

night, we discussed the kind of numbers it seems that girls never do, not the number on the scale, but the numbers on our bank statements. We talked about day rates and agent commissions, mutual funds, and retirement accounts. All of the girls had been modeling much longer than me, and because I'd been afraid to discuss how much I'd been making with anyone else, I'd just left it all in my savings account.

"Making two percent interest?" Elsie said.

"I just started six months ago!" I reminded her.

And before I could even ask, she went to the desk in the living room, took out a pen and a notepad, and handed it to me.

"Take notes, girlfriend."

Which is exactly what I did.

After dinner, we all helped to wash up. There wasn't a whole lot to do. The food *had* all come from Nobu. It was more that nobody wanted the evening to end.

"It's like we're in a girl band or something," Prageeta said. "Nobody knows exactly what it's like to be us."

I asked if anybody else was headed uptown on the West Side, but nobody was.

"Bummer," I said. "I hate to take the subway by myself."

Melody said, "It's eleven o'clock at night. Don't take the subway by yourself. Ever."

"Cabs are expensive," I said.

"Right," Elsie said. "And you make a lot of money. Not

to mention, cabs are a deductible expense."

* * *

So I hopped in the first cab I saw and listened to my messages. There was just one. It was from Chela. She said, "I just want you to know that I had dinner tonight at Asia de Cuba, at the bar, by myself. The lobster fried rice is really good. You should try it sometime."

I couldn't believe I'd forgotten that I was supposed to meet her. When did I turn into the sort of girl who blows off her best friend? The cab stopped at a red light, and there was a bus-stop ad of me, Melody, Prageeta, and Elsie. I know it was mean, but I couldn't help but think maybe I'd outgrown my friendship with Chela. Maybe the Trophy Life girls were my new best friends.

Bee-twixt and Bee-tween

The next day, I was walking down Fiftieth Street on my way to a go see when this girl I knew from high school came running up to me.

"You probably don't remember me," she said, as if high school had been ten years ago instead of six months.

"Of course, I remember you," I said.

Her name was Roberta Bailey, and her dad was some crazy-rich banker. She'd been a cheerleader, president of the French club, and prosecuting attorney in Mock Trial. She'd done a lot of things in high school, but the one thing she never did was speak to me.

Now Roberta was in my face as if we were the best of pals. She said, "I just thought there was no way *you* would remember *me!*"

"Roberta, we went to high school together for four years," I said.

"I know, but we never got a chance to hang in high school, and I always regretted that," she said. "Then I saw you in *Seventeen* a few months back, and I've been, you know, looking out for you."

"Really? What for?" I didn't mean to be a bitch, but pretending to be completely nonchalant about someone as popular as Roberta Bailey was a heck of a lot of fun.

"Well, since you're at Columbia and I'm at NYU, I was thinking that, you know, we could chair an intramural fund-raising event together. Maybe something involving fashion?"

"That would be cool," I said, trying to be polite.

"Maybe we could do some sort of student fashion show; you know, I've always been interested in modeling myself."

"Listen, Roberta, I'm late for an appointment," I said, looking at my watch. "I've got to go."

"Oh yeah, of course, I understand," she said. "You have my number, right? Call me."

Yeah, right. Like that was going to happen.

Truth be told, I hadn't thought one iota about Roberta Bailey since I started at Columbia. But back in high school, I thought about her all the time. Especially when her dad chartered this boat and had a huge graduation party that my high school pal Haylie was invited to and I was ceremoniously not. Haylie said she had asked Roberta if she could bring me along, but that Roberta had said the guest list was "limited." A limited guest list on a ship the size of the freaking *Titanic*.

I spent the night of Roberta's graduation party seeing *Space Station* at our local IMAX theater with my dad. Cool flick, but not so cool that I wasn't just a little bitter. I had hoped that one day Roberta Bailey would be sorry she had snubbed me, hoped that she'd be sorry she'd had the chance to be my friend and had dissed me big time. I used to daydream about her seeing me on *Oprah*, not on one of those shows where the guests are just pitiful and you can tell that Oprah just wants to shake them for not having the sense that God gave them. No, I was going to be on *Oprah* discussing how I came up with a cure for breast cancer, and Oprah would be giving me that "you are so damn smart I can barely stand it" smile that she reserves for people who truly impress her. The smile that says, "The next time I throw a big fabulous party at my house in Santa Barbara or on a yacht for Maya Angelou, you are soooo invited."

I used to watch *Oprah* every day after school, and it would always trip me out when she said, "God can dream bigger than you ever can." But that just goes to prove that Oprah Winfrey never told a lie. Because in all of my revenge fantasies, I never once pictured Roberta Bailey kissing my butt as we stood next to a bus-stop ad of me at Rockefeller Center. Whoever said that revenge is a dish best served cold never had the pleasure of becoming famous in six months flat.

❊ ❊ ❊

The next week, Kevin asked me to go with him to the MTV awards. We'd been talking on the phone, but between his schedule and my schedule, we'd never actually gone out.

"The MTV awards are kind of a big deal for a first date," I said.

"I hate this industry stuff," Kevin said. "It'll be good to be out with an old friend."

That's where the confusion set in. When we talked on the phone, we flirted up a storm. But when Kevin said things like I was an "old friend," I thought, Okay, I've got it wrong. I've totally misread him.

To add to the drama, the MTV awards were on a Tuesday, and I was scheduled to take a makeup of Professor Trotter's physics exam, which I'd missed because I was shooting my first Cover Girl commercial. I went to see Professor Trotter, but she wasn't having it.

"Excuse me, Professor," I said, sticking my head into her office.

"Are you not clear aboot what materials the final on Tuesday evening will cover?"

"No, that's not it," I explained. "It's just that I've got a work thing."

I could feel my face getting hot 'cause I'm not a very good liar. But I figured that walking the red carpet with Kevin was worth its weight in publicity gold. That made it a work thing, right?

Professor Trotter crossed her eyes at me. "I may be getting up in years, but I'm not an idiot. The reason you are taking the final on Tuesday night is because you missed the exam on Friday morning for a 'work thing.' Do you really expect me to reschedule the exam again? That's as far away as a puffin ever flew."

"Excuse me?" I had no idea what a puffin was or what it had to do with Kevin and me.

"That's a no, Miss Wilson. No. See you tomorrow night."

* * *

By the time I got home to my apartment, I was bawling like a baby. There was no way I could miss the MTV awards. But if I skipped the physics final, I was not going to make the Dean's List. Moreover, I was going to fail physics and have to take it again. I knew that by going to the awards with Kevin, I'd be throwing away a whole semester of hard work. Still, I called everybody I knew in the hopes that someone would say I should blow off the exam.

* * *

So I called Leslie and tried to work the publicity angle.

"Do you know how much press I would get if I showed up on the red carpet with Kevin?"

"A ton," Leslie said. "But not enough to throw away a whole semester of hard work at an Ivy League school. Come on, Bee, you're smart. Do the math."

I called Prageeta, Elsie, and Melody. None of them would back me up.

Steeling myself for the truly tough call of the day, I hit

Kevin on his cell.

"Where you at?" I asked.

"At the studio, laying down some tracks," he said.

"Can I come by?"

"What's up, Bee?" Kevin knew that I wouldn't bother him in the studio unless it was serious.

"I'll tell you when I get there."

* * *

I hopped in a cab down to the Village to the Electric Lady Studios, where Kevin liked to record. The studio had been built in the sixties by Jimi Hendrix, and all these musical giants had recorded there—John Lennon, the Rolling Stones, David Bowie, Curtis Mayfield. It was a cool space—apparently Jimi Hendrix had asked for all "soft curves and no right angles."

Kevin's crew—his band, engineers, agent, label exec, and all of his groupies—were hanging out in Studio A, so we slipped into Studio C, which was empty. It was a small room with purple velvet walls and gold sound panels. I couldn't help but notice that squarely situated above his perfect jaw, Kevin also had a beautiful pair of full lips. They were plump as pillows, and I really wanted to kiss him. He took a seat at the piano, then gestured for me to sit next to him. He began to play a song that I didn't recognize. I didn't even know he could play piano.

"That's beautiful," I said. "What is it?"

"Louis Armstrong," he said, then doing a mean Satchmo impersonation, he began to sing, "I see trees of green, red roses too/I see 'em bloom for me and you/And I think to myself, what a wonderful world."

Memo to self: heavenly moment. Gorgeous guy serenading me in world-famous record studio. Never forget how good being in like can be. Especially if you have a feeling that what you're going to say next will ruin everything.

"Kev," I said. "I can't go with you tomorrow night."

"Why not?" he asked. He had stopped playing the piano.

"I've got to take my physics final," I explained. "I had a Cover Girl commercial last week, and I missed it. This was the appointed makeup time, and I forgot all about the MTV awards, and now my prof won't let me change."

He turned back to the piano and started to play "What a Wonderful World" again.

"You gotta do what you gotta do," he said nonchalantly.

"Are you mad?"

"No, I'm not mad," he said. "I'm disappointed. I hate going to those things. I'm not even nominated, I'm just going to present an award to newcomer of the year. I wanted to have my thoroughest girl with me."

Then before I could stop the words from coming out of my mouth, I said, "You could go with my friend Chela."

Open mouth. Insert entire mentally challenged foot.

"Who?" Kevin said.

"My friend Chela. She's really pretty," I continued,

trying to dig myself out of the self-esteem hole but only burying myself further.

"Please," Kevin said. "Pretty is a dime a dozen. You're pretty and smart."

He gave me this devilish look. "You don't have a crush on your teacher, do you?"

He was playing with me. Everything was going to be okay.

"My physics teacher is a she," I started.

"That's hot," he said.

"No, it's not," I said, laughing. "Professor Trotter is a slightly cross-eyed Canadian with buckteeth and a beak of a nose."

"Okay, scratch that," he said.

"But if I do well on the exam, then I'll have a 3.8 average, and I'll make the Dean's List," I said.

Kevin turned around and stood up. He was suddenly very close to me.

"A 3.8," he said, leaning closer. "Now *that's* sexy."

Was he going to kiss me? Oh my God. But he didn't. He just winked and then showed me the way back out of the studio.

* * *

I took the exam, and despite Professor Trotter humming what I could only imagine were Mountie campfire songs the whole time, I was pretty sure I aced it. I went to bed Tuesday night exhausted but happy.

Wednesday morning was a whole other matter entirely. I got up and saw Kevin on *MTV News*.

"Kevin and Savannah Hughes," the *MTV News* announcer said, "they were all over each other at the MTV awards last night."

I turned off the TV and tried to fight back the tears. I knew Kevin and I weren't dating, but he was one of my best pals. My cute, sexy boy-who's-not-my-boyfriend pal. He could date whomever he wanted, but not Savannah Hughes. Anybody but Savannah Hughes.

* * *

I threw on a pair of sweats and went to the newsstand on the corner of Columbus and 110th. I picked up the *Daily News* and the *New York Post* and then went to H&H for a hot bagel with cream cheese. I wasn't going to make it through the day without carbs.

Back in my room, I turned immediately to the gossip pages. Kevin and Savannah were the lead item in both papers.

My cell started to ring. It was Kevin. I let it go to voice mail.

I turned on my computer and Googled "DJ Drop and Roll and Savannah Hughes" and got a gazillion hits. It was everywhere: MTV, E!, VH-1, the CW, even CNN had an item about it. C-freaking-N-N. They were supposed to carry real news, not dregs from the bottom of the gossip pool.

My phone was ringing again. Kevin. I let it go to voice mail.

I went into the bathroom and locked the door. I took off my sweats and took a hard long look in the mirror. Savannah Hughes was skinny again, and she looked amazing. I was crazy to think that I could compete with the likes of her. Kevin had probably been playing with me from the start. I'd made a small fortune proclaiming to the world that I loved my baby fat. But I didn't. Not today. I got dressed and went back to my room.

The phone was ringing. It was Kevin again. I figured I might as well get it over with.

"Hello," I said. "Fat Girl, Inc."

Open mouth. Insert all-too-familiar foot.

"What did you say?" Kevin asked.

"Fat Girl, Inc.," I said, repeating the words that were almost too painful to say. But there was some part of me that felt like if I was mean to myself first, it would hurt less when he was mean.

"Whatever," Kevin said, ignoring me. "I need to talk to you about last night. Can you come meet me at the studio again?"

"I don't think so. I've got a Lean Cuisine in the oven, and then I've got a photo shoot for Big Girl Panties that I absolutely can't miss."

"What is up with you?" he said, sounding genuinely puzzled.

I wanted to say, "You. You're what's up with me. I take my freaking physics exam, and you go to the MTV awards with a skinny model. And not just any skinny model, but a skinny model who for some reason—known only to her and God—hates my guts. You hurt me, Kevin, and I'm afraid to see you because I'm afraid you'll just hurt me more."

Instead I said, "It was fun while it lasted, Kev. Gotta love the Trophy Life girls. More cushion for the pushing, right?"

"You have lost it, Bee," Kev said. "The pictures were my fault, but all this is on you. You can't love someone more than she loves you."

And with that, he hung up the phone.

* * *

Was I right? Had he said that he loved me? Was that even what he meant? I looked at the pictures of Kevin and Savannah in the newspapers, and I knew that I had heard him wrong. He loved me like a friend—if that. He and Savannah were clearly more, much more, than friends.

What was I thinking? He had the number-one video in the country and two of those video dancers could fit into one pair of my jeans.

Leslie had warned me about this. She had said to be careful, that a lot of guys would want to get with me just to say that they had. When Kevin was driving his Lexus SUV through Times Square, did he want to give a head nod at the billboard and say, "Oh yeah, that chick, I hooked up with her."

Thank God, I didn't kiss him.

Thank God, I didn't kiss him.

Thank God, I didn't kiss him.

                                                  ✶ ✶ ✶

I was racing across campus, desperate to get home so I could get into full cry mode: BedHead pajamas, rum-raisin ice cream, daytime television on mute. I could barely see through the glaze of tears that were ready to fall, which is why I wasn't looking where I was going. Which is how I bumped right into Brian.

"Hey, Bee," he said, like we were long-lost friends.

Oh God.

"I've been meaning to call you," he said.

If I had run into Brian just twenty-four hours earlier, I would've told him where to step off. The thing is, crushing on Kevin made me sort of forget that the whole reason I wanted to be a model was to get Brian back. But it wasn't twenty-four hours ago; it was now. And just like Justin Timberlake in the video for "Sexy Back," Brian was back in my life. And he brought all of his sexiness with him.

18

Bee's Boyfriend Is Back

I woke up the next day happier than I'd been in such a long time. Brian and I were back together! How cool was that? I know he'd been a bit of a jerk, but so what? We all make mistakes. Brian had apologized to me profusely all throughout dinner last night and then on a moonlit walk to Central Park. He told me that he didn't even care that I was modeling, that he didn't need some stupid magazine to tell him that I was beautiful, he'd fallen in love with me the first moment he saw me.

"Do you remember that day?" he asked me.

I nodded; how could I ever forget?

"I was so scared to ask you out," he said as we walked down Broadway to Columbus Circle.

We got to the circle, and Brian did the most romantic thing. He hired one of those horse-drawn carriages that cost like fifty dollars an hour, and he took me for a ride around the park.

"I think I was scared our entire relationship. I knew

you were the one, but I was afraid to commit. That's why I freaked out over Thanksgiving."

Just then my cell phone started to ring. I looked at the number. Kevin. I pushed the "Reject" button, and the call went straight to voice mail.

"Do you need to get that?" Brian asked.

"Nope," I answered.

Ten minutes later, the phone rang again. Kevin.

"Someone's trying to get ahold of you," Brian said.

"No one important," I assured him. Then I switched my phone off, turned to Brian, and kissed him good night before we hopped in a cab. I was beaming the whole way home.

I know it probably seems like I jumped right back into Brian's arms. He was my first love, and I hoped, all confusing feelings with Kevin aside, that Brian would be my only love.

When we got out of the cab, he walked me to my front door and kissed me good-bye in the lobby. After all, everything about Kevin was bling, but that didn't make it real.

* * *

The next morning, in my apartment, I turned on my phone. Three missed calls from Kevin, but no messages. What did I tell you? He's as fake as a twenty-five-dollar Louis Vuitton purse from Chinatown.

There was also a message from Chela. "Number one, I forgive you for standing me up. But don't try it again.

Number two, I see you made the Dean's List. Congratulations, girl. I'm up there too. Call me. We'll celebrate."

Chela. The whole time I was with Brian the night before, she hadn't crossed my mind. But how could I have forgotten? He was the whole reason that I'd met Chela in the first place. She went out with him before I did. He'd broken her heart too. Lyin' Brian, she'd called him. I couldn't get back with him and keep my friendship with Chela too.

The way I saw it was, I had three choices. I could . . .

(1) Come clean with Chela and lose her friendship entirely;

(2) Try to keep her and Brian separated and pray that sometime before I married him, I'd find the courage to tell her and she would forgive him—and me; or

(3) Lie to Chela and tell her that I was seeing Kevin, hence using the nonexistent superstar boyfriend as an excuse for my frequent absences.

* * *

I decided to go with door number three. I called Chela back.

"Hey, girl, nice job on the Dean's List," she said.

"Thanks, C. That physics final nearly did me in."

"But you aced it, right?"

"Professor Trotter gave me an A-."

"Nice. So I take it you were hanging out with DJ Smooth and Sexy last night."

"Something like that," I said.

FYI, if you ever need to ask me a question, ask me in person. I can't lie to your face, but I can lie my butt off over the phone.

"So when do I get to meet Mr. Top of the Charts? Are you officially dating now?"

"Um, well . . ."

"Oh, don't tell me he doesn't want to meet your commoner friends. You can't go out with a guy like that, Bee."

"It's not that," I said. "It's just that he keeps these crazy hours. He's in the studio all night, then he sleeps all day. I'm lucky if I can meet him for breakfast, which for him is like three in the afternoon."

"That's cool. But you tell him I want to meet him. I'll let the chucklehead know what a Bronx girl will do if he messes with my friend."

That's the thing about Chela. She always, always has my back. And in exchange for her kindness, I was lying to her.

"Thanks, *chica*," I said.

"You'd do the same for me, right?" she said. "You'd show Alejandro how those Philly girls roll if he broke my heart."

"Absolutely," I said.

And I hung up the phone, feeling like an absolute jerk. I could just see my future nuptials now:

"Lyin' Brian, do you take this woman, Bogus Bee, to be your lawfully wedded wife?"

* * *

The next day, I had a photo shoot for face cream. It was my first beauty shoot. "Just head and shoulders," Leslie said. I was getting ready to leave my apartment when Brian called.

"Hey, baby," he said.

"Hey, yourself; I gotta run."

"Where are you off to in such a hurry?"

"I've got a shoot downtown."

"A photo shoot?"

"Yep."

I was still following Leslie's rule and was always early for my call time. I looked at my watch; I had to go.

"I want to come with you," Brian said. "I've never seen a professional shoot before."

I thought about it for a second. People had friends stop by shoots all the time. It was probably no big deal to take him with me. It's not like there wouldn't be a dozen people running all over the place.

"Okay," I said, looking at my watch again. "Let me give you the address, and I'll meet you down there."

"No way, we'll go together," Brian said. "I'll be there in ten minutes."

Waiting ten minutes would still get me at the call early. So I said okay, then hung up.

Half an hour later, when Brian arrived, I was bouncing off the walls.

"Let's go," I said, turning my face when he leaned in to kiss me.

"Don't be mad; it's just that I thought I should shower and shave. You never know, they might want to shoot us together, the hot young couple in love."

This made me a little uncomfortable; no one was going to be taking Brian's picture. But why not? He was good looking. Was I turning into a model bitch?

* * *

At the shoot, I introduced myself to the photographer, a guy named Oscar Perez, who I'd never worked with before.

"You have beautiful skin," he said, touching my face. "Today will be easy."

"Hey, hands off my woman," Brian said, making a joke.

"Oscar, this is my boyfriend, Brian."

A flash of concern, or something a lot like it, crossed Oscar's eyes. But then he smiled and shook Brian's hand. "Pleased to meet you," he said. "Why don't you take a seat while we get Bee into hair and makeup?"

Andy and Syreeta were both there, waiting for me.

"Slept in, huh, girlfriend?" Andy said, nodding to Brian, who was following Oscar's assistants around and playing with different lighting equipment.

I took a seat in the chair. Syreeta said, "You should get changed first."

"What am I wearing?" I asked. "It's a beauty shot, right?"

Syreeta handed me a white cotton sarong with Velcro across the top.

"Your gown, madame."

"Cool," I said, stripping down in front of them. One thing about being a model is that you can't be shy. There are too many people around to get weird about changing rooms, and none of them is paying attention to you anyway.

I was just about to take my bra off when Brian poked his head into the makeup room.

"You know, I was thinking maybe you could do some sort of benefit show for Amnesty International," he said.

I have no problem using my model powers for good, but I was in the middle of a job.

"Brian," I said, as sweetly as I could manage. "Can you wait for me outside?"

"No problem," he said, walking away.

"This is why you don't bring your boyfriend to a photo shoot, sweetie," Andy said.

"Is he doing something wrong?"

"No, he's just in the way, ruining the vibe."

I took a deep breath. "The vibe is cool," I said. "Let's do this."

* * *

Andy gave me this ridiculous weave, with big loose curls. Syreeta gave me beautiful, flawless, golden skin. I sat on a box while Oscar used an eight-by-ten camera to pull in close on my face, neck, and shoulders. A manicurist had done my nails in a pale pink, and Oscar encouraged me to bring my hands gracefully into the shots as well.

For the first hour, everything was fine. Then Brian started to act up again. He stood next to Oscar saying the stupidest things like, "Do you recycle your film canisters? I think the PVC of all that plastic is probably pretty major. Maybe you can approach the magazines you work for about going zero, reducing the environmental impact of your shoots by planting a certain amount of trees for every shoot that you do. I know some people at Go Zero; I could hook you up."

Oscar looked miserable, but Brian kept talking. "I mean, you seem like a smart guy; do you really want to leave such a big carbon footprint with what's supposed to be your art?"

I tried to gesture to him to stop, but it's hard to be subtle when you're wearing a cotton towel, you're surrounded by klieg lights, and there are half a dozen photo assistants, stylists, and art directors watching your every move. But Brian kept going on about the environment, global warming, the time he had dinner with Al Gore and Leonardo DiCaprio. Finally Oscar said, "Hey, man, I'm going to have to ask you to go."

Brian was livid. "You're kicking me out? Do you not know that this is my girlfriend? There would be no photo shoot without Bee."

That whooshing sound you just heard? It was all of the air being sucked out of my lungs. In other words, I was horrified.

"Brian, I'll meet you later," I said quietly.

"Okay, baby," he said, making a big show of coming over onto the seamless backdrop and tongue kissing me in front of everyone, even though I was in full makeup.

"I will see *you* later, sexy," he said. "And make sure you get some lunch. Don't let these people try to starve you. I know how this industry is."

And on that note, he left.

Oscar stepped behind the camera, looked at me through the lens, then said, "Your makeup is ruined. We'll have to do it all again. Let's continue after lunch. I'll see everyone in forty-five."

Syreeta handed me a bathrobe, a big fluffy one, like the kind they have in really nice hotels. I walked over to the catering table, grabbed a plateful of pasta salad and two brownies (I know, I know), and then found a quiet corner to sit by myself.

I was midway through my second brownie when I heard Leslie's voice.

"Just because they're only shooting you from the neck up doesn't mean you can eat like there's no tomorrow," she said.

I looked up, and there was my superagent, catching me in some very un-supe-like behavior. She looked gorgeous.

But you've heard me talk about Leslie. Gorgeous is a given. If she ever looks like crap, you'll hear it on CNN.

"Am I in trouble?" I asked, confident that Oscar must've called her.

"For what?"

"Oh, nothing," I said, relieved.

"I mean, you don't get 'in trouble' because your jerky college boyfriend comes to the photo shoot and disrupts a multi-million-dollar ad campaign."

Oscar *had* called her.

"There's a reason we don't bring boyfriends and girl-friends to shoots, Bee."

"But the stylists and hair and makeup have people drop by all the time."

Leslie sighed. "Those are industry friends. People in the business who know how to behave."

"I got it."

"So who was that guy?"

"My boyfriend," I said.

She looked puzzled. "DJ Go Drop Dead?"

I shook my head. "I was . . . hanging out with Kevin. But this is my *real* boyfriend, the guy I was dating before I became a model."

"The one who dropped you right before Thanksgiving?"

Had I even mentioned Brian to Leslie? The woman had a memory like a steel trap.

"We got back together," I said.

"After you had a billboard in Times Square and were on the *Today* show."

"Technically, yes."

Leslie gave me a hug. "Be careful, Bee."

"That's what you said about the rapper."

"That's what I have to say about all the men in your life now that you're famous. You're seventeen years old, and when you're a hot young model, it's even harder to know who to trust."

I picked up one of the Polaroids that Oscar had taken to test the light. Who was the girl in the photographs? The one who smiled like she had all the answers. I wanted to be her.

Bee-sieged

The next day, I had lunch with Leslie at the Four Seasons, which is like something out of a movie. Doormen in top hats. Flower arrangements bigger than a person. Super-swank.

I know she's my agent and agents are supposed to be semi-evil. But I'd already seen that Leslie had a sweet side too. Don't get me wrong, she could be gangsta. Nobody negotiated harder than she did, but she was also cool. Like the big sister I never had. Or rather the older, British, size-two sister I never had.

I ordered the soup and salad. Leslie ordered the same.

"Well, Bee, I've got some good news and some bad news. What do you want to hear first?"

"Good news, always," I said, resisting the urge to gobble on the warm bread at the table.

"Should I have them take away the bread?" Leslie asked, reading my mind or my stomach.

"Yes, please," I said.

Leslie gestured for the waiter, and he came and took the bread away.

"The good news, Les," I said.

"The good news is that Mattel wants to do a Barbie doll in your image. They're going to call her Bee. She's going to be Barbie's plus-size cousin."

"Get out!" I screeched.

"I'm not going anywhere without my fifteen percent," Leslie said, cracking a very typical agent joke.

I sat there for a second in shock. My own Bee doll. Of all the things I ever imagined when I began modeling, this was the one thing that had never crossed my mind.

"How did this happen? Are they doing all the Trophy Life girls?"

"Nope," Leslie said. "Just you. In some ways, we have your parents to thank. They really like that your name is Bee. Apparently, some exec at Mattel saw you on the *Today* show a while back and thought, 'This could be Barbie's cousin Bee.' Then she saw your 'Sweet Sixteen' editorial in *Teen Vogue* and she loved seeing you in all those frothy prom dresses. It made her think that her initial instinct, that you could be a fashion doll, was spot-on. They have an artist working on some prototypes and sketches. I'll have them messenger them over to you."

For once, everything was right in my world. My grades had slipped a little from first semester, but as my adviser kept telling me, a few Cs never ever hurt anybody. Not even when that person was premed. Brian and I had gotten back together, and because I was so busy with work, Chela hadn't found out. If I wasn't working, I still met her on Friday nights to go salsa dancing at the Copa. I just never mentioned Brian. And if Brian asked what I was doing on Friday nights, I told him I was working. I believe the Latin phrase for this is *lying out of both sides of mouthus.*

"This is amazing," I said, for once telling the absolute truth. "One day when I have a little girl, I can give her a Bee doll to play with."

"Are you kidding?" Leslie said. "My niece has already put in an order for twelve. She wants to give them as a birthday gift to every girl in her class."

I started to cry. I just couldn't believe it.

"You said there was some bad news," I said.

Leslie handed me a pack of tissues.

"The licensing agreement at Mattel is iron clad. You're going to make a flat fee for this doll, but there's no royalties."

I dabbed my eyes. "That's the bad news? I don't care about royalties."

"Well, I do," Leslie said, flashing her super-evil-agent grin. "When I saw your contract, I nearly shed a few tears myself."

* * *

The next day, I was hanging out with Brian when a messenger arrived. The package was from Mattel. I put it on my desk to open later, in private. As much as I was psyched about having a Bee doll, I was kind of shy about talking about it in front of Brian. The modeling stuff brought out a weird side of him. On the one hand, he decried the whole fashion industry as "shallow, superficial, and out of touch with the real issues in the world." At the same time, he seemed to want to be all in it. It was confusing.

"What's in the envelope?" he asked.

"Oh, just some papers."

He picked up the envelope.

"What kind of papers would you get from Mattel?"

I didn't want to tell him, but why should I have to hide such good news from my boyfriend? The boyfriend I wanted to marry and someday have a baby with so that she could play with her very own Bee doll.

"They're making a doll of me," I said.

"A Bee doll?" Brian was incredulous. I understood. I was still a little in shock myself.

"Yeah," I said, opening the envelope.

"Is she going to be your size?"

I don't know why, but the question really hurt my feelings. He was a guy; what did he care about what size the Bee doll was?

"Yep." I took three or four doll molds out of the bag as well as some sketches.

Brian picked one up. "They don't have faces. They're kind of creepy."

"I know," I said. "They want me to pick the shape I like the best."

"Well, this one has the best shape," Brian said, picking up a doll with a Jessica Biel booty and Shakira abs.

"I like her," I said.

"But this one looks the most like you," he said, picking up the doll with a pear-shaped body: small breasts, medium waist, big hips.

"Okay," I said. "But I like this one."

I picked up the doll with the Jessica Biel booty and Shakira abs. I mean, who cares, right? If you looked at her arms, her hips, and her thighs, the doll was still clearly plus. And I'd been working out with a trainer for nearly three months now. By summer, I fully intended on having a sculpted booty and if not a six-pack, then at least a two-pack or a three-pack.

"Well, you aren't shaped like that. You should be honest," Brian said.

Ouch. That's all I have to say about this particular subject is "ouch, ouch, and double ouch."

"If I want the Bee doll to have a banging body, then that's my right, Brian. It's just a doll," I said, snatching it away from him.

"Whatever," he said, getting up. "I'm just saying do you believe all this stuff about loving your plus-size self or is it just an act? I've got to get to class."

He was all excited out because he had been selected for

this super-exclusive senior seminar in international-conflict resolution. It was being taught by someone I should be listening to, Kofi Annan. But all I could think about after Brian left was his little sarcastic comments.

❊ ❊ ❊

As a gift for landing the Mattel contract, Leslie had gotten me tickets to this new series that MTV was doing called *MTV Amped*. It was like the opposite of *Unplugged*. In *Amped*, they were going to take artists who normally played acoustic instruments and give them electric guitars and have them do their same songs, all amped up. The first artist on the roster was Norah Jones. I was really psyched to snag the tickets, and of course I asked Brian even though I knew Chela was the hugest Norah Jones fan. It just seemed like more of a boyfriend-girlfriend kind of thing. We had backstage passes too, which was seriously cool.

The only problem was that Brian seemed to think he was going out on a private date with Norah Jones. He must have changed clothes at least half a dozen times. He kept saying, "How do I look?" And I'd say, "You look great." And he'd say, "Yeah, but I'm meeting Norah Jones, and she's sexy gorgeous. Did you know she's half Indian, and she's like some sort of special ambassador to the UN?" I wanted to say, "Hey, buddy, I'm kind of a big deal too. I've got a billboard in Times Square." But how do you say something like that without sounding like a typical self-centered model?

We were supposed to arrive an hour before taping started, and we got there about five minutes before the show was to start. When we arrived at the studio on the West Side, I gave our names at the backstage door. The publicist, Juliet, came running up to me.

"Bee, I'm so glad you're here; we're just about to start," Juliet said, then, turning to the girl with the clipboard, "You're supposed to radio me when the VIPs arrive."

Juliet led us through the crowded studio audience and to the front row, where Norah's band was setting up.

She approached two people and said, "I'm sorry, these seats belong to Bee Wilson. I'm going to have to seat you in the back."

Two girls got up, and Brian and I sat down.

"Thanks, Juliet," I said. "These seats are amazing."

"No problem, Bee. I loved your spread in *Glamour*. Do you have my card? If you want tickets to anything, call me."

Then she walked away.

"This is unbelievable," Brian said, staring at me.

"I know. I can't believe we're going to see Norah Jones rock out on the electric guitar."

"No, I mean that you're considered a VIP now. That woman all but kissed your feet."

"It's not that extreme," I said.

"Uh, it is," Brian said. "I mean, I'm just really glad we got back together."

Just then, Norah came out onto the stage. It was a good thing too 'cause I honestly didn't have a thing to say to Brian.

* * *

The next day, I was shooting my very first television commercial without the Trophy Life girls. It was for Bond Number 9 perfume, and we were shooting it on Long Island. It's such a long way out there—two hours if the traffic's not bad—that I invited Brian to come with me even though Leslie said not to. I made him promise to stay in my trailer all day, and I figured afterward, we could take a romantic walk on the beach and maybe have dinner at B. Smith's, overlooking the water, in Sag Harbor. Things had been a tad tense with us. Everything he said felt so hurtful, but I figured it was just me being supersensitive. I'm working so much and I'm studying so hard. I'm a total stress ball! Somewhere deep down inside, I was probably still paranoid that Brian would leave me again. A beautiful Friday out near the beach would fix everything. I would work a little, then I'd play a little. That's what it's all about, right?

When I got to the set, I met the director. She was this really cool British woman named Karen Greene. I'm not trying to say anything, but has anybody noticed that people from England dominate the fashion scene? It's like they decided since they couldn't colonize the world, they'd focus on designing clothes, becoming photographers, and being big-time agents, so they can boss around models instead.

I had Brian safely sequestered in the trailer, and I was all dressed in my first outfit, this really cool off-the-shoulder cocktail dress by Rachel Roy. It was supersoft jersey, kind of like a souped-up version of the sweatshirt the girl in the eighties movie *Flashdance* wore. When I was in high school, my friends and I used to Netflix *Flashdance* all the time, until finally my dad got me the DVD for my birthday. Dressed in this short gray jersey dress with one shoulder exposed, it was all I could do not to start jogging in place and singing, "She's a maniac! Maniac on the floor! And she'd dancing like she's never danced before!"

Karen explained that I was to get in the car, spritz myself with the perfume, and then pretend to drive. Because this was the thing: The car was a three-hundred-thousand-dollar baby blue Bentley, and they'd have a car in front of me, towing it, so that I wouldn't actually have to drive the thing at all.

Still, I was nervous as all hell. A three-hundred-thousand-dollar car. I was only seventeen. My license said I couldn't drive without at least one adult in the car.

"Don't worry, luvvie," Karen said. "We've got plenty of insurance if the car gets scratched. That said, don't scratch the car."

She took a long look at me. "You know what, Bee? I love your red hair, but I think it's clashing with the car. Let's put you in a blonde wig." So they did. They put me in this super-straight blonde wig, then they pulled it up into a massive French twist. It was amazing to see how much hair can change your personality. All of a sudden, I felt very slick, very triple *C* (calm, cool, and collected).

When I came out of hair and makeup, Karen was ecstatic. "I love it," she said. "Now you're a Hitchcock blonde."

* * *

It was different being filmed by live cameras than it was for still photography. Every movement had to be totally smooth. I only had one line to say, but I must've said it a hundred times. Each time, Karen had a different instruction. "A little more fierce, Bee," she'd say. "This time, give me a little purr in your voice. Like you're ready to rev this motor and go."

As many different ways as I humanly could, I said, "Bond Number 9 is my perfume because while I love a fast car, I like to take it slow."

After about four hours, Karen announced that we were breaking for lunch. They always have huge catered spreads at shoots, but I knew that then the goodies on display were sure to be too high in calories. So I'd ordered sushi delivered to my trailer. As Melody says, "It's not impossible. But it's really, really hard to get fat eating sushi."

It was kind of a strange concept. Everyone in the fashion industry thought we were the fat girls because we were plus size. But we worked really hard to stay in shape. I was now meeting my trainer, Jenisa, every morning at six A.M., six days a week. Leslie had arranged for me to meet a nutritionist, who insisted I keep a food diary. Having to write down everything I ate was tough. Having to fax her a copy every night was tedious. But it was a fresh slice of hell having Jenisa, a size-two drill sergeant from Georgia, call you up and say in her thick southern accent, "Watch ya step, missy. Because I have *read* your food diary, and I can see plain as day that yesterday ya had waffles!"

When I got to the trailer, however, Brian had eaten my sushi.

"I was hungry," he said, shrugging. "And bored. I can't believe how much time these fashion people sit around doing nothing."

I wanted to correct him. *He* was sitting around doing nothing; *I* was actually working. But I knew how it looked from the outside—photo shoots are long and sometimes they are boring.

"I want to see that new Don Cheadle documentary about Darfur," Brian said.

"We'll go as soon as we wrap," I said, wondering if I should ask a production assistant for another serving of sushi or just grab a smoothie and call it a day.

"That's a sweet ride they have you driving," Brian said. "Is that a Bentley?"

"It is," I said, nibbling on banana chips.

"Look," he said. "I'm sorry I ate your lunch. That was very unsupportive of me. I'll go to the catering truck and get you a Caesar salad and a Diet Coke. How does that sound?"

"Great," I said. I know that I could have asked an assistant to go for me, but I was too embarrassed. It was sweet of Brian to offer to go for me.

* * *

About fifteen minutes later, I heard a huge crash. I rushed to the window, and there was Brian, in the driver's seat of the Bentley. The air bag had exploded, which probably saved him from some sort of major head injury. But, honestly, I think his block head could have survived any kind of trauma. Apparently, he'd gone out to get my lunch, wandered over to the car, and noticed that the key was still in the ignition. He had this crazy idea that he was going to drive the car to the local television station and make a statement about luxury cars and how Americans used more than our fair share of the earth's natural resources.

What he didn't know was that the car was attached by a tow line to the truck in front of it. The line was hidden so it wouldn't show as we shot the commercial. So he turned the car on, mashed the gas, and kapow. The front of the car was completely smashed in. Karen was turning all shades of purple, and before I could say, "I'm sorry," my cell phone was ringing, and Leslie was reading me the riot act.

"I spoke to you about having your boyfriend at shoots," she said.

"But Karen said there was insurance," I said hopefully.

"There is insurance to cover authorized drivers," Leslie said. "But the fact is that you have not only destroyed a three-hundred-thousand-dollar vehicle, you have put an end to the day's shoot, which will cost the client another half-million dollars by the time they send the cast and crew home, replace the car, and reschedule the shoot."

"When's the shoot rescheduled for? I'll come anytime. I'll do it for free."

"You'll do no such thing," Leslie said. "Because you are fired. Now go home."

I went back to the trailer to change. Brian, for all of his attempts at grand-theft auto, was sporting a very small Band-Aid on his forehead but still complaining like he'd been the victim of some heinous crime.

"My head really hurts," he said. "I might have a mild concussion."

"I'm the one whose head hurts," I said. "I haven't had any lunch, and, oh yeah, by the way, I was fired."

"Who cares? It was just some perfume commercial," he said.

All of a sudden, I looked at him and for the first time, maybe ever, I really saw him for what he was. A nice guy. A guy who was so smart about so many things. But a guy I really didn't care to spend any more time with, at all. Not when he could so casually break my heart. Then take me back. Then risk ruining my modeling career—the one really good thing I had going. I suddenly realized if I had to choose between Brian and modeling, I'd choose modeling.

"Look, Brian, it's over," I said. "I don't want to go out with you anymore. Getting back together was a mistake."

He looked stunned.

"You're breaking up with me? Because of some over-priced, non-fuel-efficient car?" he said.

"It's not because of the car," I said, sitting across from him in the tiny trailer. I could feel myself crying, and I knew that it was everything—Brian, being fired from the commercial, the whole lot of it.

"We're just not a good fit," I said.

"You know what, you can't be breaking up with me," Brian said, his voice turning snarky. "Girls like you don't dump guys like me. You only got lucky because there's this whole trend to make people feel good about themselves. You were in the right place at the right time, and now it's given you a big head."

There's a quote from Maya Angelou that I scribbled in my journal once, and I've never forgotten it. She said, "When people show you who they are, believe them the first time."

Brian had shown me who he was, and instead of just walking away from the experience, I became obsessed with getting him back. Now that he'd said all those mean things about me, I knew that I needed to walk out the trailer door and keep on walking. Which is exactly what I did.

I went over to Karen, apologized for the car, and then

asked if a teamster could drive Brian to the train station. I'd just opened the door to the town car for the long ride back to New York when Brian came running after me.

"Hey, where are you going? You're my ride," he said.

"I'm sorry," I said, smiling as sweetly as I could. "I'm just too fat. There's no room for you and my big model ego. You'll have to take the train."

Then I got in the car and asked the driver to go. We had a long drive back to New York, and I had a whole mess of crying to do.

20

Oh, Bee-have!

Even though I totally blew the Bond Number 9 shoot, Leslie got me booked for a music-video shoot for a British band. It turns out Aunt Zo had a recital in London the same weekend, so we were able to fly together. I was kind of bummed—to say the least—about the breakup with Brian, but when it came down to it, I realized that while he was all the things that I loved about him—handsome and smart and politically conscious—being around him always felt like work. I was always trying to seem like I was something that I wasn't. It was like Chela always said, "Do *you*." With Brian, I couldn't really do me.

Besides, I hardly ever saw Aunt Zo, so it would be fun to hang out with her. I managed to get Zo upgraded to business class, and we were chilling, with plenty of leg room, catching up on all that had been going on.

The stewardess came around to ask for our meal orders, but Aunt Zo had already packed a feast from Zabar's: roast-beef sandwiches with blue cheese dressing, tomato-

and-cucumber salad, kettle chips, and Godiva chocolate.

"Zo, the food in business class is actually not that bad," I told her.

"I know, but I'm a musician. I'm used to traveling like a gypsy. I bring my own food. I'm prepared to be routed and rerouted."

She looked so beautiful. For years, she'd worn her hair in this pixie cut, but she was letting it grow out. Andy, my hairdresser, had given her this cool scissor cut and her layers were very rock 'n' roll.

"You look edgy," I said, admiringly.

Zo laughed. "Good. Maybe I'll run into Eric Clapton in London."

"Don't any of your musician friends know him?"

"Probably. Speaking of friends, you haven't mentioned Chela in ages."

I fidgeted with my personal video screen.

"You two have a tuss up?"

I guess *tuss up* is as good a term as any for the fact that I'd gotten back together with Brian and was sneaking around behind her back. I'd dumped him, but I'd been so busy with work and school, I hadn't gone dancing with Chela in weeks.

"Something like that," I said.

"It can't be easy for her, your sudden fame when the two of you used to be so close."

I rolled my eyes. "What am I supposed to do, call her

up and say, 'Sorry I'm no longer lonely and pathetic and able to hang out with you 24/7. I've got a life now, and I've been kind of too busy to be your chubby sidekick.'"

Zo gave me a stern look. "Is that how she made you feel?"

"That's how I felt."

"But do you think she purposefully tried to keep you down?"

This gets back to the whole lying thing. If we'd been on the phone, I could've been deceitful: Yes, I would've said, Chela is gorgeous and I always felt like a big cow compared to her. But sitting next to Aunt Zo, ten thousand feet above the ground, I couldn't lie. I had to tell the truth.

"No, she was a great friend to me."

"Then call her."

"Okay, I will," I said, and I meant it too.

* * *

The agency set us up at this cool hotel, where on check-in, you could have a goldfish delivered to your room. We named ours Ben, in honor of Aunt Zo's new boyfriend, who was a clarinetist in the touring company of *Wicked*. Zo and I had dinner at Yo! Sushi, a funny restaurant where you sit at a counter and this conveyor belt of sushi goes around and around. You just pick what you want as it comes by. I had an early call the next day, so I went to bed while Aunt Zo caught up with some of her musician buddies. "We're night owls by nature," she said as she took off for her second dinner date of the evening at ten P.M.

The next morning, I showed up at the studio and met the director and her team. It was kind of a weird situation. I'd never been in a music video before. I knew that the lead singer of the band—they were called Guess Again Girl, had been in New York and seen my billboard in Times Square. Jess, the director, had this concept to shoot me as a painting in all the museums from all over the world. The lead singer, Garrett, would wander in and out of museums and sing to me in the paintings. It sounded pretty cool— there was going to be lots of blue screen, lots of elaborate costume changes.

"It's going to take bloody forever," Jess said, explaining why it was such a challenging shoot.

"No problem," I said. "I'm used to waiting around."

It was a whole new crew of people to get used to. But there must be some law that the hair and makeup people become a model's best friends. Because in no time, I was chatting to the lead hair guy, Karl, and the lead makeup guy, Mickey, as if they were long-lost friends.

The first setup was a reproduction of John Singer Sargent's *Madame X*, a painting Aunt Zo had actually taken me to see at the Met in New York. It was apparently the Paris Hilton videotape of its time, although it's just a painting of a woman in a long strapless black dress. Karl put a red glaze in my hair, and then Mickey gave me a fabulous glamour look. Three hours later, I was ready. Three hours after that, the band showed up.

"Sorry we're late," Garrett said, kissing Jess on the cheek. The other guys in the band mumbled apologies as well.

Garrett came up to me, looking like a nineteenth-century painting, and actually got on one knee and kissed my hand.

"My muse," he said. "I'm Garrett, and those other geezers are Lance, Mario, and Elliot."

I waved hello to the band.

Mickey gave all the guys a dusting of face powder, and literally ten minutes later, they were ready to go. No makeup. No hair. No stylists. I'd always thought that the scruffy-rock-star thing was contrived. That it took ages to get that lived-in look. Not these guys.

The set was made to look like a museum-gallery room, the genius of which, Jess explained, is that all over the world, gallery rooms look the same. One set would work for all four locations. They were just changing the paintings, the extras, the costumes.

The song was called "Picture in a Frame," and since it was off of the upcoming Guess Again Girl album, I hadn't heard it yet. In the video, Garrett wanders around the gallery, singing the song. There are all these extras looking at paintings and sketching, while the other guys in the band play their instruments in the corner and everyone pretends not to see them. In the first setup, Garrett is singing to a reproduction of Sargent's *Madame X*. In the second setup, the painting comes to life and I'm there, leaning on a chestnut side table, trying to look elegant and swank and 150 years old. I'd never had anyone serenade me before; that was kind of nice, even if there were dozens of people standing around and watching us.

The next day was even crazier. I was meant to be a portrait by Velázquez come to life. The museum was the Prado and the painting was *Queen Margherita on Horseback*. The queen part was cool. I had this fluffy white collar around my neck, this amazingly intricate burgundy brocade gown, and while I didn't wear a crown (apparently not horseback-riding gear), they pulled my hair up in a bun and covered it with this sexy little silk net. The problem was, of course, the horse. She was lovely, her name was Paula, and she was golden brown with white spots and either amazingly well behaved or drugged out of her horsey little mind. Either way, I was happy. The thing is that in my long brocade gown, it took three people to hoist me on top of Paula, and once I had mounted her, I discovered this fear of heights I'd never had before. I was terrified I would fall or that Paula would start bucking and I would fall and she would trample me. So when Garrett started singing, I apparently had this dazed and terrified look on my face. I loved the song and had no problem looking at him dreamily before. But I could barely hear him now as he sang:

"You're just a picture in a frame/I'm no match for your

games/I bet the house, how could I win?/Now I'm out and the other guy's in/All I've got's a picture in a frame."

Jess called cut, then she came over to me. "What's wrong, Bee?"

"I'm just a little nervous, that's all," I said.

"You look beautiful," Garrett said, coming up to me and kissing my hand for the second day in a row.

"The horse is perfectly tame. Have you met her trainer, Louden?"

Louden, a scrappy-looking old guy in a tweed cap and a plaid vest, came over and shook my hand. His accent was heavy.

"Don't you worry about Paula. You could trust her to carry a newborn baby safely to London tower on her back."

"Uh, okay," I said.

Jess suggested we take a break, and the three photo assistants helped me dismount the horse.

I was sitting in the corner, trying to do the yoga breaths that Melody had taught me, when Elliot, the guitarist, came over to see me.

"You going to be okay, Bee?"

"Yeah, I'm fine."

"I brought you some potato salad."

FYI, just because I'm a plus-size model, doesn't mean I eat like it's going out of style.

"It's ten o'clock in the morning," I said.

"My mum made it," he said, pouting a little.

I took the bowl from him and ate one spoonful. It was awful. I put the spoon down.

"It's delicious," I said.

"Well, eat up, then," Elliot said. "Finish this bowl, and I'll give you a second."

Which made me wonder, would "yum" have been a less enthusiastic but still polite response?

He sat there staring at me, so I ate the whole bowl. When he jumped up to get a second, I said, "No, please, I'm stuffed."

Jess called us back into the shot, and I started walking toward the set.

Twelve hours later, I woke up to find myself in my hotel room. The room was dark, and I could barely make out Ben the goldfish in the bowl next to my bed.

I wandered out of the room, and Zo jumped to her feet. "You're up, thank God. What happened to you, Bee?"

That was a very good question. What had happened to me?

"I don't know. I was at the shoot . . ."

"And you were spooked by the horse? The photographer thought maybe you had a panic attack and blacked out. Of course, she also implied that you might have been on drugs, but I told her you were clean. Speaking of which, Leslie's called about a dozen times, so give her a call, okay?"

I was thinking about what Aunt Zo had said about drugs, then I realized that the last thing I remembered was Elliot giving me that bowl of potato salad and being so insistent that I eat it, even though it was ten in the morning.

"Zo, is there some sort of drug that you could put in potato salad?"

She raised an eyebrow. "You can put almost anything in anything. Why?"

I told her about Elliot and his "mother's potato salad." She agreed that it didn't sound right. We called the hotel concierge, and they arranged for us to go to the hospital.

An hour later, we had the toxicology report. I'd been given a horse tranquilizer. The doctor looked at me and said, "You are very lucky that you are not ze skinny girl. Your body could metabolize ze drug in a healthy way. Ze skinny girl might have had a heart attack and died."

Of course, what I heard him saying was that I was big enough for a horse tranquilizer. Aunt Zo and I argued about this the whole cab ride back to the hotel.

"He said I was a horse," I said.

"He said that you're lucky to be alive," she said.

"Because I'm a horse."

"Because you're lucky," Zo said. "Look, Bee, I won't do this with you. This 'am I fat?' thing. You're gorgeous. You have always been gorgeous. And now you're getting paid a ton of money and have become quite famous for being gorgeous. You're my favorite niece. The fact that you are my only one is immaterial. Please don't let this modeling thing turn you into a self-hating 'do I look fat in this?' person. It's petty and it's boring."

Those were harsh words coming from Aunt Zo. She hated petty people, and she hated boring people more. She'd never, ever used either word in reference to me.

"By the way," Aunt Zo said, "my concert was tonight."

"Oh no," I said.

"Oh yes," she said.

"I'm so sorry you canceled it because of me."

"There'll be other concerts."

I reached across the cab and hugged her. Amazingly, she hugged me back. Memo to self: Shape up and earn Zo's respect again.

❖ ❖ ❖

Back at the hotel, I called Leslie in New York. She was furious at me for passing out at the shoot until I explained that I'd been drugged.

"Well, you're about to get your first taste of the British tabloid system," she said. "Tomorrow's *Daily Mail* is running an article that implies you stole the tranqs from the trailer in order to get high."

"Oh no," I said.

"Oh yes," she said.

❖ ❖ ❖

The next morning, it was worse than I'd imagined. There was a picture of me looking terrified on top of

Paula. The headline read, "BOVINE BEAUTY STEALS HORSE PILLS FOR CHEAP THRILLS."

The British paparazzi were waiting outside of my hotel, and when I got to the lobby, the hotel manager said, "I wouldn't go out that way, ma'am." He said he'd order the car to come back around the side entrance, but they were there too. I was used to cameras flashing in my face, but not forty or fifty at a time. The hotel manager threw his jacket over my head and shoved me in the backseat.

"Um, thanks," I said just before he slammed the door shut.

"Tell the agency you need some sort of security," he said. "Protect you from the wolves."

* * *

Call time was eleven A.M. I arrived on set, with a lunch packed by Aunt Zo. She'd run out to the food court at Harrods and prepared a feast for me. If I could've kept it under lock and key, I would have.

Jess took me aside and apologized for the band's behavior. She said they were all going to apologize to me as well, and she hoped that we could get through the rest of the shoot without incident.

Garrett and the guys arrived, and they shuffled over to me, one by one, like they were naughty schoolboys preparing to be spanked. I accepted their apologies, though I decided that Elliot was a toad. He seemed to be holding back a laugh when he muttered, "It wasn't a very funny joke, was it?" Which I guess in England passes for an apology. But when I went to the bathroom, someone had taped a dozen copies of the front page of the *Daily Mail* to the bathroom wall. I wonder who?

21

Just Bee-stly

The next day, I got dressed up as Queen Margarita once again. Maybe it was the residual tranq in my system, or maybe after the day I'd had, I was up for anything, but I mounted Paula with no problem and managed to get through Garrett's song with a loving expression on my face.

Since we'd missed a day's worth of work, we were pulling a double shift. Just before dinner, we set up for the third shot. In this one, I was to be portraying the *Toilet of Venus*, by Rubens. In the painting, the woman is looking in a mirror held by an angel. She also had one breast showing, which Leslie had already told them wasn't happening. Karl put extensions in my hair, and I wore this white silky nightgown. There was a little girl dressed up as an angel, all set to hold my mirror. Her name was Gwendolyn, and she was gorgeous: big beautiful eyes, dark curly hair. She was also a little monster. She started off by sticking her tongue out at me. No biggie. I stuck my tongue out back at her. I thought we were just playing around.

Then she started pulling my extensions out. Karl had glued them instead of sewing them in since we were pressed for time. Every time she yanked one, I screamed in pain. Finally, Jess took both the monster and the monster's mother aside and gave them a talk about professional behavior.

Gwendolyn came back to the set with a little angel smile on her face.

"I'm sorry," she said.

"It's okay," I said, reaching down to give her a hug. But she pulled away from me.

"I'm sorry you're a drug-addicted cow," she said, and then she kicked me.

Kicking me when nobody was looking, which was every five minutes or so, became Gwenny's game for the rest of the shoot, which lasted until two the following morning. I know that I'm vastly overpaid as a model, but on the Guess Again Girl shoot I was earning every penny.

* * *

The final day of the shoot was an easy one. I was to be Madame Monet in Renoir's *Madame Monet Reading Le Figaro*, which meant that I got to wear a gorgeous pale blue gown, lie on a chaise lounge, and read a French newspaper. Well, look at a French newspaper and pretend to read. Still, the shoot took all day. Jess wanted to get plenty of angles so that she'd have a lot to work with in the editing room, so we did a thousand variations on this one simple shot. By the end of the day, when she called wrap, I thought if I never heard "Picture in a Frame," it would be too damn soon.

Afterward, everyone went out to dinner at a cool restaurant called Spoon. I was nervous about eating anywhere in the vicinity of the band, but Jess assured me she'd keep Elliot and the other guys far away from my food. I sat at the other end of the table with Karl and Mickey, the hair and makeup guys, who referred to themselves as BQs: bitchy queens. They made hilarious jokes about everyone in the restaurant, and I laughed all night long.

After dinner, Garrett asked me if he could walk me back to my hotel. I figured it was okay. After a guy sings you a love song two hundred times, you start to have friendly feelings toward him. He was cute and he knew it. In the restaurant, girls kept coming up to him and asking for an autograph. Even walking down the street, I thought it was funny to see people doing double takes as they realized who they'd walked by.

I'd never been to London before, and central London at night was like something out of a movie. We walked past the most perfect town houses: cream-colored bricks with shiny jet black doors and wrought iron balconies and gates. There were a million little parks and greenery everywhere: grass, trees, shrubs. No wonder all the cool American celebrities were moving to London: Madonna and Gwyneth Paltrow and Angelina Jolie and Brad Pitt. It was like New York, but older and different and so pretty.

Garrett told me about how he'd grown up north of London in Manchester. Apparently, they have a really great soccer team, which they call football. He told me how he'd named the band Guess Again Girl after his high school girlfriend dumped him and told him he'd never amount to anything, which I thought was pretty cool. He asked me if I had a boyfriend, and I told him that we'd just had a pretty nasty breakup. He said, "Those must be going around. I just had one of those too."

When we got to the hotel, I was telling Garrett all about the goldfish the front desk had given us for our stay and how we'd named him Ben, after Zo's new boyfriend.

"I'd love to meet Ben," Garrett said, touching my hair.

"Well, my aunt Zo is sleeping," I said, covering, as if Zo ever went to bed before midnight.

"Fine, I'll get us another room," he said, walking toward the check-in desk.

"I'm not going to bed with you," I said bluntly.

"What? You've got morals now?"

"I've got morals always."

"How American of you, to sit up on your high horse. . . ."

"You should know better than to talk to me about horses, Garrett." I glared at him, remembering the night Zo missed her concert because of his friends and their stupid practical joke.

"So you let me fly you to London, make you the star

of my most expensive video yet, and you don't think I'm entitled."

"Entitled to what?"

"Entitled to some of that ass that I paid for."

You know how if you ask your parents what the sixties were about, they always say, "Sex, drugs, and rock 'n' roll?" If someday my kids ask me what the early twenty-first century was about, I'm going to tell them, "Sex, drugs, and bullshit."

"Garrett, let me break it down for you. You did not fly me here; your record company did. You did not pay my modeling fees; your record company did. And neither you nor your record company paid for any ass. Now run home, like a good little boy."

He looked like he was going to say more, whether to insult me or cajole, I couldn't tell. But then Aunt Zo walked in the front door and came over and gave me a hug.

"How you doing, Bee?" she said, giving Garrett the once-over.

"Just fine," I said.

And on that note, we turned and left him standing there. But even as we walked away, I could hear a girl asking him, "Excuse me, are you Garrett Phillips from Guess Again Girl. . . ."

* * *

"Well, guess again, girl," Leslie said.

"Uh-oh."

"Someone put out an underground video of the same song. Black and white. Not so flattering of you. I think it's got to be the guys in the band, but the record company is claiming total innocence."

"Is it going to be on MTV?"

"No, thank God. But it's on YouTube."

"Okay, Les. I'll check it out."

I went over to my computer and typed the URL in. There I was on the front page, a really unflattering shot of me trying to eat that wretched potato salad. The video was called "The Picture Won't Fit in the Frame."

It was grainy, black and white, but it was definitely me. Someone had filmed every time I had something to eat, then they'd spliced it together as one giant food fest. The grand finale? Me falling flat on my face after eating that horse tranquilizer. Instead of the last chorus of the song, there was a girl's voice singing, "Food coma, food coma, food coma," until there was this electronica crescendo and a fuzzy fade-out.

My phone rang. I checked the number. It was my dad.

"Honey, I need to talk to you." He sounded bad.

"What's wrong, Dad? Are you okay? Is Mom okay?"

A million thoughts ran through my head. Had my mother been in a car accident? Did my father have cancer? Did my mother have cancer? What could be so wrong?

"We're okay," Dad said, but his voice said different.

"You're lying to me, Dad," I said. "I'm getting on a

flight first thing in the morning. I'll be in Philly by the afternoon."

"Bee, you don't have to do that."

"Well, I will, unless you tell me what's wrong."

"I don't know how to say this," Dad said. "I just never thought I'd ever have to worry about something like this."

My heart was beating so fast. I couldn't bear the thought of something bad happening to my dad. Or my mom. But especially my dad.

"Dad, just tell me," I said in the most mature, grown-up voice I could manage.

"Bee, are you on heroin?"

What?

"Bee, are you there?"

"I'm here, Dad."

"I need you to be straight with me. Are you using heroin?"

"Dad. Where would you get an idea like that?"

"This guy at my office showed me your music video on YouTube."

Did I mention that my dad is a scientist? And that all of his coworkers are geeky science nerds? Of course, they spend their downtime trolling Websites like YouTube.

"Dad, that's a bootleg video that the guys in the band put out as a joke. The real video is on MTV. It's really pretty. I'll get a DVD made for you."

"But why did you allow them to photograph you eating

like that? And then at the end, you just passed out."

So I told him the whole story.

"I worry about you, Bee. This business you're in sounds dangerous. What if Zo hadn't been there?"

"Every business has its ups and downs," I said. "I can handle it, Dad. Nine times out of ten, everything is on the up-and-up and completely professional. It's just that there are a lot of jerks in modeling. I'm learning how to put them in their place."

I thought about how I'd turned down Garrett that night in London when he just expected that I'd go to bed with him because he's the lead singer of some stupid boy band. Guess again, boy.

"Bee, ever since you started this modeling thing, we hardly ever see you. What do you say your mother and I drive into the city on Sunday and take you out to dinner? I just need to see you, make sure my baby girl is okay."

"I would love that, Dad. Dinner would be really nice."

22

Bee-gin the Bee-grime

When I got back to New York, Leslie called me into a meeting at her office. I was terrified that she was going to drop me from the agency's roster. When I arrived, she didn't greet me with the fashion kiss on both cheeks that I was used to. In fact, she never got up from behind her desk.

I sat down on one of the chairs in front of her, and she said, "Look, Bee, I'm going to get right to the point. I've been doing some investigating as to why the Guess Again Girl guys would pull such an awful prank on you."

"And?" My palms were sweaty, and I tried, discreetly, to wipe them off on my skirt.

"Apparently, Garrett, the lead singer, had insisted on directing the video himself. His version starred another model. Guess who?"

"Savannah Hughes?"

"Bingo. I haven't seen it, but apparently it consisted of them drunkenly pub crawling all over London. It was black and white, out of focus, and the label deemed it unusable. Enter a new director who chooses a new model."

"Me."

"Savannah put the guys up to the bootleg video because she feels like you're all over her turf."

"So what are we going to do?"

"Unfortunately, there's not much I can do," Leslie said. "It's a cutthroat business. This is where it gets nasty. But we don't have any proof that she's behind this, and she's technically not the one who drugged you."

I'd gone from feeling nervous to being mad. What was it going to take to put Savannah Hughes in her place?

"So why'd you call me in here, Les?"

"Just to let you know what I'd learned and to advise you to be careful."

"That's it?" I was really angry now. "The video is being downloaded like a thousand times a minute on YouTube. My own father thinks I'm on drugs!"

Leslie sighed. "The video makes you look like a druggie. Which in our business is not uncommon. But you've been caught on film. I hate to tell you this, but we've actually had a few clients cancel bookings over it."

"So what do I do?"

"Ride it out," Leslie said. "I need you to be über-professional at all of your bookings. Be early. Be friendly. Don't take too many trips to the bathroom—that's bound to promote gossip. And do your best not to get a cold. If you start sniffling, the rumor will explode."

I couldn't believe what I was hearing.

"As a matter of fact, just to make sure you don't get sick, I want you to see my herbalist and my acupuncturist. Stop and see Caroline on your way out, and she'll make sure that they take you this afternoon, tomorrow morning at the latest."

"So I try not to get sick, but what if the bootleg video sticks?"

"The record company is releasing the real video in two weeks," Leslie said. "I hear that it is absolutely stunning. Hopefully, it will go to number one on *TRL*, and everyone will forget about the bootleg."

"And if it doesn't?"

Leslie's smile was forced and she looked uncomfortable. "We'll cross that bridge when we get there, Bee."

"No, I want to know now. Worse-case scenario."

"If something big doesn't hit, then, well, it's been nice working with you."

She looked at her watch. "Don't you have a shoot this afternoon?"

I did.

"Then, we're done here."

She picked up the phone and started dialing. I thought that Leslie was actually starting to like me. Hadn't she hugged me that day when Brian had acted like such a jerk at the shoot? I felt the same way I did when Brian broke up

with me the first time. Like I was being dumped by someone I really, really liked, and I had no idea why. I stopped
at Caroline's office to get the number of the herbalist and
the acupuncturist, then I walked out onto the street. It was
one of those inappropriately sunny days when the beauty
of the day seems to mock your own inner misery.

* * *

That afternoon, I had a shoot out in the Hamptons.
Andy and Syreeta were on the shoot too, so we all rode out
together in a town car. It was fun; we had a picnic basket
from Zabar's, and the two-hour ride went by in no time.
But when we got to the beach house where we were supposed to do the shoot, we found out that the stylists had
pulled the wrong sizes. Nothing fit and not just because I'd
had a bagel *and* a chocolate-chip muffin that morning. The
stylists had pulled a size ten. I'm a twelve to fourteen.

"What are we going to do?" I asked the photographer.
His name was Marc, and we'd worked together before. He
was really sweet, and I felt really comfortable with him.

"Well, it's Saturday, so all the showrooms are closed;
we can't pull new clothes," Marc said. "Can you just try
stuff on? Maybe some of it's cut a little loose."

Callie, the stylist, was, by the way, completely unre-
pentant. "Size ten *is* a plus size," she kept saying to anyone
who would listen.

I tried everything on, and it was an exercise in humili-
ation. Three tops fit, which was some sort of small miracle.

But I couldn't get any of the dresses over my hips.

"We'll just have to cut them at the seams and clamp them at the back," Marc said. "We'll shoot you head-on and no motion shots."

"On the beach?" I asked. "But won't people be out there?"

"We'll put up a scrim to protect you," Marc said.

* * *

In the end, in order to get a photo of me with the ocean in the background, Marc needed to pull the scrim, which is kind of like a thin curtain. This meant anyone walking on the beach could see that from the front, the dresses looked perfectly fine. From the back, they were split wide open and clamped, with cold metal clips, to my bra and panties. I was so embarrassed. It was really hard to pose.

"Come on, Bee, you're giving me dead-fish eyes," Marc said.

I tried to think happy thoughts: Kevin kissing me in the lobby of my building, salsa dancing with Chela at the Copa, being at Prageeta's engagement party in London.

"Much better, Bee. I know this is hard, but focus and we'll get it done," Marc said, snapping away.

I smiled until it physically hurt.

Then all of a sudden, I heard the familiar whirr of a camera clicking away, but the sound was coming from the wrong direction. I turned around and there were five paparazzi, taking photos of my ass.

Marc and Andy chased them away while Syreeta got me a robe as quick as was humanly possible. Interestingly enough, Callie was the only person who didn't seem surprised by the ambush. In fact, she was whispering into her cell, a big grin on her face.

I didn't have to guess who she was talking to.

"Hello, Savannah?" I said, grabbing the phone away from Callie.

"Oh, Bee, darling," she said. "I've been seeing you everywhere. I do mean *everywhere*. Someone just e-mailed me a picture of your ass in a too-small dress. Overexposure is a terrible thing. Didn't your agent teach you that?"

"Don't worry about me," I said. "You're the one who ought to be watching your back."

I tossed the cell phone at Callie and resisted the urge to chuck it at her head. All I needed was to end up in a court-appointed anger-management course like Naomi Campbell.

* * *

This completely fabricated feud I was having with Savannah Hughes was going way too far. She'd been a supe as a regular-size model, now she was the princess of plus: thereby proving that sometimes you really do get to have your cake and eat it too. She'd been on the cover of EVERY SINGLE MAJOR WOMEN'S MAGAZINE. I was nothing compared to her. Why she chose to chugalug the Haterade was beyond me.

Now my reputation was in the toilet and now I was losing work. All because I'd managed to annoy a girl that I'd met exactly once in my entire life. This didn't even make sense. My whole modeling career had felt like a fairy tale. But I guess that's the thing about fairy tales: they're pretend, a dream. Eventually you've got to wake up and deal with real life.

Which is *exactly* what happened when I came back from the shoot in the Hamptons to find Chela waiting outside the front door of my apartment building. She was dressed in this really cute zigzag knit dress and some leather peep-toe shoes. As usual, she looked amazing.

"I'm so glad to see you," I said when the town car dropped me off. "You'll never believe what happened to me at my shoot today."

I went to give her a huge hug, but she just pushed me away.

"I saw you on TV last night," she said.

"What? More mess about that Guess Again Girl underground video." I groaned. "It's like a pimple that just grows and grows until it covers your entire face."

But Chela's eyes had no sympathy. She looked really cold. "I'm not talking about Guess Again Girl. I'm talking about 'Norah Jones Amped' on MTV. I saw you in the front row with Brian, holding hands, and how he was kissing on your neck. The camera was on you two half the time. How could you, Bee? After what he did to you? After what he did to us?"

I tried to make up a lie. "I got the tickets so last minute and I ran into him at the library, so I asked him to go. But it's not what you think. He *is* a complete jerk. I'm not even speaking to him."

"We had a pact, Bee," Chela said. "And I don't believe that you even tried to call me. You never call me anymore now that you're this big-time model. It's like you forgot how much I believed in you from the very first day. All I can think is your self-esteem must've been in the trash to go crawling back to Brian. But my self-esteem is intact, and I don't need friends like you who don't appreciate how dope I really am."

And on that note, she turned around and left. Which was just as well because I didn't have a whole lot to say. All I know is that for the first time in a long time, I was lonely. Really lonely.

I went upstairs and changed into my favorite pink-and-brown flannel pajamas. They had been a gift from my aunt Zo a few Christmases back, and for a while, they were the only non-global-village clothes I ever owned. Now I had a closet full of designer dresses, shoes, and bags, but I didn't feel like the glamour-puss I thought girls with stuff like that must feel like.

I called Ollie's and ordered a bowl of wonton soup for dinner, and I was really surprised to see that my old pal, Dewei, was the delivery guy.

"Long time no see, Bee," he said. "I heard you're a famous model now. My cousin says you have a billboard in Times Square."

"Yeah, something like that," I mumbled.

"Well, I haven't seen the billboard, but I told my cousin, Bee doesn't order takeout every night anymore. She's got a life," he said.

I paid for the order and gave him a twenty-dollar tip.

"You're not ordering every day is bad for business but good for Bee," Dewei said. "Maybe you order every once in a while. Like tonight. For old times' sake."

"Yep, old times' sake," I said as I locked the door behind Dewei.

I took the takeout container into the kitchen and put it in a blue-and-white Chinese bowl that Chela had bought for me as a birthday gift from Pearl River market.

"If you're going to eat takeout, then at least put it in a nice bowl," she had said. "Food tastes better when it's not eaten out of cardboard and plastic foam."

And she was right. I crawled into bed and flipped on Turner Classic Movies. Believe it or not, they were playing *Flashdance*. I thought, Maybe my life's not all gone to hell in a handbasket, like my aunt Zo always said. But despite the fact that Jennifer Beals was dancing like a "maniac, maniac on the floor," I sensed that things weren't going to go as well for me.

It was like when I was a kid and my father used to take

me to this bowling alley in Philly that had really old video games. I loved to play Ms. Pac-Man, and sometimes, I could make one quarter last for hours. But inevitably, there came a point when my luck ran out, and I always hated the moment when that bright blue message came on-screen: GAME OVER. Could I have really lost my modeling career and my best friend in one fell swoop just like that? Was it really game over?

23

Plan Bee

Except for going to class and stopping by the student center for smoothies or falafels, I pretty much spent the next few days in my pajamas watching movies. *To Catch a Thief* came on, and I finally got what the Bond Number 9 director meant when she wanted me to portray a Hitchcock blonde. But every time I watched Grace Kelly drive around the Italian Riviera in that supercute car, all I could think about was Brian and how he'd smashed up the car and finished off the job of ruining my life that Savannah Hughes had started.

I called in to the Chesterfield agency to see if they had any bookings for me, but Leslie didn't even get on the phone. Her managing director, Caroline, basically gave me a polite version of "Don't call us, we'll call you." Which, as you can imagine, really sucked.

I was really, really tempted to ease the pain by sticking my face into a barrel of Häagen-Dazs, but I got up and made myself a cup of green tea, which I drank with exactly two Fig Newtons. Brian was wrong. I was not fat. I had the potential to be fat, and if I skipped one more session with my trainer, Jenisa, then it would be a slippery slope. But I planned to pick up with her on Monday. Even if I didn't get any more modeling gigs. I liked the girl who I saw every time I took a taxi through Times Square (I have to admit, I always requested that route, no matter where I was going). I was a curvaceous babe, and I had every intention of staying that way.

That said, I really, really didn't want to go out. But that Friday night, Prageeta and her fiancé, Hanif, were hosting an engagement party at the Mandarin Oriental Hotel near Central Park. I called my aunt Zo to see if she wanted to go with me, but she had a show. I was tempted to call Chela, but I didn't want her to think I was using her. So I decided to go by myself. I'd make a quick appearance, say hello to the Trophy Life girls, then be back at home, and in my pj's, by the eleven P.M. movie, which I happened to know was going to be *Mystic Pizza*, which kinda rocks.

The party was a masked ball, so after my last class, I stopped at a costume shop on Broadway and got a kitty-eye mask and glued a hot pink bindi to the center of it. I was wearing a white tank top with a glittery design and a long hot pink skirt and glittery sandals. Prageeta is always saying, "Pink is the navy blue of India," so I figured I'd fit in just fine.

I took a cab to the hotel lobby, where two men in tuxedos were holding clipboards. I gave them my name and they ushered me in.

Another doorman led me to a private elevator and hit the button that said "Penthouse." When the doors opened, we were in the penthouse itself. There were huge floor-to-ceiling windows, and there must have been two hundred people milling about. I spotted the Trophy Life girls immediately. It helps that models are tall when you're scanning a super-crowded room. Elsie and Melody were in a corner, near a giant piano. When I got closer, I saw that Diana Krall was playing it.

"It's Diana Krall," Elsie whispered.

"That's pretty cool," I whispered back.

I asked where Prageeta was. Melody laughed and gestured to the corner, where Prageeta was talking to Bill Clinton.

"That is the former president of the United States," I said, in a painful elaboration of the obvious.

"You think?" Elsie said, laughing.

"Go over and say hello; I know she'll want to see you," Mel said.

"No way," I said. "I'm not going to interrupt Bill Clinton."

"Well, I will," Elsie said, grabbing my arm. Did I mention that Bill Clinton is also on Elsie's list of top-ten favorite people? I was beginning to think that if we stayed at this party long enough, we'd hit all ten.

"I'm going to throw the bouquet right at my girls," Prageeta said. She looked gorgeous in a purple sari halter top and a long skirt embroidered with purple and green peacocks.

"Me? I'm only seventeen!" I said.

"In India, girls get married even younger," Prageeta said.

"At this point, I'd settle for a great boyfriend," I explained.

"School first, career second, boyfriend third," Elsie said. "Let's go check out the sunset."

"Yes, the terrace is magnificent," Prageeta said.

I gave her another hug.

"I love my Trophy Life girls," I said.

"And we love you right back," she answered before Hanif whisked her away.

I was talking to Elsie about whether facials really help your skin. She swears by them, but Melody won't let anyone near her face. Then Elsie saw number nine on her top-ten list of favorite people, Jon Stewart.

"I'll be right back," she said.

"No problem," I said.

They were serving canapés on the terrace, and a champagne fountain spouted the bubbly stuff as if it were water. But the main item on the menu was New York itself.

It's so easy when you're in the midst of things to think of New York as this gray, ugly mess—especially when it's winter or raining and you're stuck on the subway on the smelliest car ever and it seems like there's trash everywhere and all the really nice places have tuxedoed doormen, like the ones downstairs, who you think will never, ever let you in. But when you do get in—to a fancy party or even just to the observation deck on the Empire State Building after you've been standing in line for *hours*—you can stand from someplace high up and see that the city is magic. Pure magic.

I watched the boats along the Hudson, the people skating, running, and walking through Central Park, and I wondered, Did I use up my share of the magic? Does everyone get a little box: a few nights of dancing salsa with a friend like Chela, listening to Kevin talk about Cantor's theory of sets in Starbucks, then seeing his album debut at number one on the Billboard charts, getting my own moment the spotlight as a Trophy Life girl. Was I greedy to want more? To want it all?

I was thinking about it, taking it all in, when I noticed that Prageeta was standing next to me.

"Look at this view," she said, leaning on the railing. "I'm going to miss New York."

She and Hanif were moving to London.

"So you're just going to give modeling up completely?" I asked.

She shrugged. "It was never my calling or anything. It was just something fun to do while I waited for my grown-up life to begin."

"But doesn't it make you feel grown up? The creativity of the designers, the amazing places we get to travel to, seeing your picture in a magazine or on TV?" I asked. I knew I sounded superficial, but the more I talked about it, the more I realized that although I'd fallen out of love with Brian, I was really in love with modeling.

Prageeta smiled. "My family and Hanif's family have known each other for *generations*. I've had a crush on him since I was probably eight years old. The fact that I'm going to get to be his *wife*, that we will continue this link, and that someday our children will also be linked, that excites me. Besides, I haven't told anybody except for Hanif, but I've been doing some writing myself."

"Wow," I said.

"Just some short stories about being a woman in India and New York and London," Prageeta said. "I'm very excited about moving to London and having the time to work on them."

"I have the perfect title for you," I said.

"And what is that?" she said with a smirk. "Because *Bride and Prejudice* has already been taken."

"*Pink Is the Navy Blue of India*," I said.

Prageeta smiled. "That's pretty good." Then she kissed me on the cheek. "We must make our own decisions," she said. "But remember that this is a tough business. Very few do it for the rest of their lives. Every model I know who is happy has a passion that has nothing to do with physical beauty. Melody has her yoga and photography. Elsie dreams of that seat on the New York Stock Exchange. I know you're premed, Bee, but I don't sense the dream is deeply rooted in your heart."

I winced a little. Just a few months before, Kevin had made the same observation.

"You're only seventeen; you'll figure it out," Prageeta said. "Why don't you come inside so I can introduce you to some nice Indian guys? A couple of them are really good looking, and *all* of them can dance."

"In a minute," I said, and I turned to watch Prageeta go back to the party. I envied her for being so beautiful, for being so smart, for having it all sorted out.

Even though it had grown chilly, I stood outside for another half an hour. I was gobsmacked by the river. I kept thinking that the way it flowed, moving so quickly and powerfully through the city, was like my modeling career. That day in Dean and DeLuca, when Leslie handed me her card, it was like modeling was my river. I could jump in and see where it took me or I could sit and watch it pass me by. But it was my river.

24

Humble Bee

I guess the thing is that I thought when I got chosen to be a Trophy Life girl, I was in there like swimwear. I mean, I had a billboard in Times Square. But if there's one thing I've learned as a baby supe, it's that while shooting to the top can be really easy, it's much harder to stay there.

When I first started modeling, all I could think about was Brian and how if he could see me in a magazine, looking extra fly, then he'd want me back in an instant. It never occurred to me that maybe I didn't really want him. It was more like the idea of him—a cute upperclassman with a mission to save the world.

The first time Chela and I went out dancing, she had said there's a Spanish expression that goes "*un clavo saca otro clavo.*" One nail takes out another nail. Well, modeling took out the Brian nail. But I'm not sure what's going to take out the modeling nail. I used to think that modeling was all about conceited girls, the pretty ones who were always so popular that now they got paid to stare into mirrors and pose in front of cameras all day long.

But now that I've been on the other side of the camera, I know that modeling is so much more. I mean, look at me. I was never the most gorgeous girl in the room. Then I got dumped and depressed and became a really, really good customer at Krispy Kreme, and the top modeling agent in the world picked me out and signed me up. She said, "We need more girls like you, who represent real women."

I thought my life was over when Brian dumped me, but it turns out, it was just starting. And the most exciting part of it all wasn't the fancy trips or the town cars or the free clothes, it was the day that Savannah Hughes cut a big chunk of my hair, and with a new haircut, I discovered the real Bee—the one that loved a really cute pair of kitten heels as much as she loved fluid mechanics.

For months, I'd been living like Dr. Jekyll and Ms. Hyde: premed student by day and baby supe by night. (Okay, more like baby supe by afternoon and early evening.) But now it was time to get back to the basics.

I'd actually fallen so far behind in physics lab that I had to hire a tutor of my own. I also applied for few summer internships: a Barbara Jordan health-policy internship in D.C. and an apprenticeship with Doctors without Borders in Kenya so that I could actually use my Swahili. My mom even got her boss, who's apparently some do-gooder superwoman, to write me a recommendation letter. "I'm really proud of you, Bee," she said when I called to tell her about my plans for the summer.

I hadn't heard from Leslie Chesterfield in a while. She never officially dropped me, which is just as well because I didn't need a whole panel of judges and Leslie Chesterfield holding a picture that was NOT mine to realize that I was no longer in the running to be America's Next Top Model.

The commercials were still going strong, and I continued to get residual checks every other week. Finally, I decided to call Elsie for some advice. I was kind of nervous. I saw Melody twice a week for yoga classes, but she was like total Omgirl. She never talked about work. Calling Elsie took more guts. She would know for sure that I'd been blacklisted and wasn't getting any work.

Prageeta had quit the business, but Melody and Elsie were everywhere. Aerin Lauder had chosen Elsie to be the new face of the Estée Lauder fragrance line; it was the kind of rich cosmetics contract that plus girls never get. I mean, the previous faces of Estée Lauder had been Elizabeth Hurley and Gwyneth Paltrow! And ever since some exec at Nike had heard that Melody was a Zenned-out human pretzel, she'd been doing an exclusive campaign with them alongside all these cool athletes like Michelle Wie and Serena Williams.

I, on the other hand, was a loser and had fallen back to the ranks of Poindexter from whence I'd come. But I had all this money in my savings account making 3 percent interest, and I knew that Elsie, more than anyone, would know exactly what to do with it.

"Um, Elsie," I said after punching in her number. "I was wondering if you wanted to meet for lunch sometime, so I could get some financial advice from you?"

"Sure," Elsie said. "How about today?"

"Um, okay," I said.

"I'll meet you at Pastis at one thirty," she said. "I'll make a rez."

Then she hung up the phone.

* * *

It was already ten A.M., which gave me a full two and a half hours to obsess about what to wear and how to answer if she asked what I'd been up to. I decided to wear a pair of cute jeans, a pair of leopard-print Louboutin wedges, and a red halter top with my red Kelly bag. As for what I'd been up to, I would not tell a lie: I'd been studying, not working, and it looked like, with the help of my tutor, I was going to make the Dean's List.

I got to the restaurant fifteen minutes early because no matter what, I could still hear Leslie chirping, "Better to be early than late, Bee," in my ear.

When Elsie arrived, looking gorgeous in a white crotchet minidress and a big floppy hat, she took off her sunglasses and gave me a huge hug.

"Bee, where have you been?" she said. "I haven't seen you since Prageeta's engagement party."

Now was the moment of reckoning. So I told her how

my career was pretty much over.

"Well, first, my ex-boyfriend crashed this really expensive Bentley on the Bond Number 9 shoot," I said.

She nodded. "Heard about that."

"And you know that Savannah Hughes was totally hating on me," I said.

"Ugly is as ugly does," Elsie said.

At this point, I started to feel so sad and anxious, all of my words came out in one big nonsensical rush. "Well, Savannah put out this underground video of me with the guys from Guess Again Girl, and I got in so much trouble. Everybody thinks I'm a drug addict, and I'll never book another modeling job again!"

The waitress was hovering, so Elsie took a quick look, then put the menu down in a move that I recognized as the thirty-second rule. If you stare at a menu for more than thirty seconds, you're bound to choose something fattening. So the idea is you keep your eyes on the soup-and-salad section, pick one, and then put the menu down before you change your mind and order something that your hips will regret.

Elsie ordered a frisée salad and a bottle of Perrier with lime. I had totally been planning to order the steak frites, which, of course, came with a ginormous side order of fries. However, being with Elsie kind of shamed me into ordering healthy, so I ordered a frisée salad too. But just to show that I no longer cared about the modeling world or my figure, I ordered my salad with a poached egg and lardons, which is just a fancy French word for little pieces of bacon.

I was glad to get the ordering out of the way because I was anxious to get back to my pity party. Since Chela wasn't speaking to me, I hadn't really had anyone to vent to, and Elsie was a good listener.

"So anyway, like I said, this video is a total nightmare and it has totally ruined my reputation—" I was mid-vent when I just started crying, and no matter how hard I tried, I couldn't stop. At first, it was just tears, but you know how sometimes you're crying so hard, your nose starts to run too? Well, it was a full-on snot fest—worthy of one of my father's grossology exhibits at the science museum. But not worthy of a fancy restaurant like Pastis. So I ran off to the bathroom to deal with the leakage problem I was having with my eyes and my nose.

When I came back, Elsie said, "Bee, I was trying to tell you, but you didn't let me get a word in edgewise. I just saw the Guess Again Girl video on VH-1, when I was getting ready to come and meet you. You look totally gorgeous in all of those scenes from paintings. I thought you'd invited me to lunch to celebrate."

To say that I was in shock would be a gross understatement along the lines of saying that Ashlee Simpson had a "little" plastic surgery.

I reminded Elsie that I'd actually invited her to lunch for financial advice. The smile on her face was so big, you'd think that I'd just told her Adam Levine from Maroon Five had walked in to the room, Adam Levine being number eight on her list of ten favorite people in the world.

While we chowed down on our frisée salads, she explained all this stuff about mutual funds, IRAs, Roth IRAs, exchange-traded funds, fixed-income securities, and private banking.

I didn't understand a word of it, but she promised to send me an e-mail explaining everything along with the name and number of her broker.

"I fired my last broker," she said, scowling. "When I told him that my goal was to buy a seat on the New York Stock Exchange, he told me a pretty little girl like me could just marry a man with an exchange seat."

"He didn't!" I said.

"He did!" she said.

And the way we went back and forth like that for a good five minutes reminded me of Chela and how she'd say, "Get out!" And I'd say, "No, you get out!"

Elsie insisted on treating for lunch, making me swear that in the future, when I paid, I'd keep all of my meal receipts for deductions. Then we made plans to get together soon. She wanted to take me to the stock exchange in the morning for something called the ringing of the opening bell. Elsie was so stoked about the stock market, it was pretty thrilling to realize that I wasn't the only model geek out there.

We kissed good-bye on both cheeks, fashion style, then I hailed a cab home. For the first time in a long time, I didn't ask the cabdriver to drive me through Times Square. I didn't need to see a billboard of myself to remember what it was like to just be *me*.

25

Queen Bee

When I got home from my lunch with Elsie, there was a message from Leslie. "Beatrice, darling, call me," she said in a breezy tone as if it hadn't been nearly a month since I'd heard from her.

I called her back, happy to have news from the modeling world but happy that I hadn't been sitting around waiting desperately for her to call.

"Your video is going to debut on *TRL* at number one this afternoon," Leslie said. "But that's not all. *Sports Illustrated* has decided to use a plus-size model for its swimsuit issue for the first time *ever*."

"And?"

What did I care about some stupid sports magazine?

"And I sent over your book last week, and they've narrowed down their decisions to two models," Leslie said.

"I'm one of them?" I asked.

"Yes, you and Savannah Hughes."

I sighed. "You know what, Leslie? I really appreciate it and I'm not going to lie. The phone not ringing has been a first-class bummer. I miss modeling, and I'd love to work with you again as long as it doesn't interfere with chem lab. But I couldn't care less about some sports magazine for guys, and I want to stay as far away as humanly possible from Savannah Hughes. The girl has chopped off my hair, had me drugged, and sent the paparazzi to photograph me half naked. She's not right in the head, and frankly, I'm a little bit afraid of her."

Now it was Leslie's turn to sigh. "*Sports Illustrated* is not just some sports magazine for guys. It's a publication with a sterling journalistic reputation and the awards to back it up. The swimsuit issue is iconic. It's never been just about pretty girls in bathing suits. This is how a model goes from being merely a girl with buzz to being a bona fide supe. It is the most prestigious cover in the industry, and every girl who has graced the cover is not only guaranteed a million dollars' worth of bookings for the year to come, but she sets the standard for beauty in the industry. The *SI* cover was the turning point for Cindy Crawford, Elle MacPherson, Tyra Banks, Heidi Klum, Daniela Pestova, and Marisa Miller."

"Oh," I said. Because what could I say to joining that legendary rank of supes and making a million dollars during my sophomore year of college?

"I understand that Savannah Hughes has proven herself to be an unstable individual, which is why I myself will accompany you to the interview," Leslie said. "But I urge you to consider this opportunity if you ever meant a word you said about your curves being so winning and wanting teenage girls to have attainable body ideals. This is not just any old go see; you have to go in and give them everything you've got. Are you committed?"

I was.

"Very well," Leslie said. "My car will pick you up at nine. Get some rest."

❊ ❊ ❊

You're not supposed to wear makeup to a go see; the idea is that the client wants to see your face as a blank canvas. But when I called Andy and Syreeta to tell them about my meeting with *SI*, they insisted on coming over the next morning to hook me up.

They arrived at seven A.M., and even though I'd gotten used to early calls, I still wasn't especially cheerful first thing in the morning. Andy was another matter entirely.

"The glam squad is here!" he announced as soon as I opened the door. He had bags and bags of hairpieces, straightening irons, curling irons. I'd seen the whole kit and caboodle, but never in my own house before.

Syreeta came in behind him with a bag of organic blueberry muffins. "Just eat the top," she advised. And while Andy fussed with my hair, she made us all a big pot of green tea.

Syreeta never goes anywhere without her music, so she had Leona Lewis blaring from her iPod, and the whole event started taking on a party mood.

In the end, Andy gave me a really simple hairdo. He clipped my bangs so they were on the short side and then hot curled the rest of my hair so it fell in ringlets around my head.

Leslie hadn't mentioned anything about actually modeling a swimsuit at the interview, but Syreeta assured me that they were going to ask me to try one on. "It's the cover of *SI*, girlfriend," she said. "They're going to want a peek at the goodies."

So she waxed my legs. OUCH. OUCH and, oh yeah, DOUBLE OUCH. And rubbed them with Skin So Soft. Then she mixed a handful of glitter with the oil and rubbed it into the area right above my bra. She called it my "décolletage." Which I think is French for the tops of your boobs.

I wore a purple peasant top with a long gold Temple St. Clair necklace, some khaki capris, and these really fabulous purple-and-gold kitten heels that I'd gotten at Bottega Veneta.

When Leslie came to pick me up, she said, "You look very nice." Which in Leslie language translates to, "You are one babelicious model, and I'm happy to be your agent."

❊ ❊ ❊

When we arrived at *Sports Illustrated*, they took me in to see "the team." There was Doug, the photographer; Steph, the cover editor; Frankie, the stylist; and Malia Mills, this really cool swimsuit designer who was going to be designing all of the swimsuits in the issue to custom fit the plus model that they chose. Did I mention that with the exception of Malia Mills, they were all English? It was all I could do not to run from the room screaming, "The British are coming! The British are coming!"

I was standing in a boardroom, and even though they were all sitting, no one offered me a seat. I felt a little bit like I was on the witness stand, but I did what Prageeta always called the red carpet pose: one leg slightly in front of the other, hands relaxed at your sides, head held high, spine straight.

"So tell us about yourself, Bee," Steph said.

"I'm a second-semester sophomore in premed at Columbia," I said. "I'm from Philadelphia, and I'm an only child."

"And what do you like to do when you're not modeling?" Doug asked.

"What I *like* to do is go salsa dancing and listen to hip hop and hang out with my friends," I said. "What I actually do is try to cram makeup labs in for chemistry and physics. I'm trying to make the Dean's List this semester, and quantum field theory is kicking my ass."

"Speaking of ass," Frankie said, smiling, "what is your greatest asset?"

I thought about saying, "My booty," but ever since I'd

gotten caught lying to Chela, I'd been all about telling the truth. So I said, "My greatest asset is my brain."

There was a lot of whispering, and everyone looked surprised. It's over, I thought. Savannah Hughes wins again.

Then Malia Mills spoke. "Bee, I've brought one of my swimsuits with me. Would you mind trying it on and giving us a little walk?"

"Not at all," I said, smiling.

* * *

I went into the hall bathroom and tried the swimsuit on. It was a one-piece. Thank God. White, not the greatest for hiding bumps and lumps, but it was backless, which was nice. I took a good look in the mirror, and I liked what I saw.

I was a little nervous about the walk. I'd never done catwalk before. Leslie always said that there was no way she could book me for fashion week with my school schedule. I stood outside the room for a few seconds, doing the three-part yoga breath that Melody had taught me. Then I opened the door to the room and strutted my stuff.

I tried to remember everything that my modeling pals had taught me. Prageeta had always said take big steps like you're an Amazon goddess stomping through a village of little people. So I did. Melody always said to keep your spine straight, but not stiff. She said your spine is actually a beautiful instrument but one that most people never learned to play. So I tried to use my spine when I walked, swaying it just a little from side to side like a palm tree in a breeze. Elsie always said never lose eye contact with the photographer. It's like when billionaires do business: They're always looking to see who blinks first. So even though I was feeling my jelly belly jiggle, I never looked away from the casting team, and I smiled, not too big, not too small, hopefully, hopefully, just right.

"Thank you very much, Bee," Doug said.

I went back to the bathroom, changed, and went back in to shake everyone's hands. Possibly the biggest go see of my entire career, and it was over in less than twenty minutes.

❊ ❊ ❊

On the way out, Leslie and I passed Savannah Hughes in the hallway. She had lost even more weight, and I was torn between being jealous and thinking that she was way too skinny to be a plus-size supe. I said hello. But she was doing the cold-and-frosty thing and pretending that she didn't see me, which suited me just fine.

26

Just Bee-chy

They picked me! They picked me! I feel like some sort of Oscar winner whose speech is so long that they start playing the music and cutting her off. Leslie called me that very afternoon.

"Congratulations, Bee," she said. "You will be the first plus-size model to be on the cover of *Sports Illustrated*'s swimsuit issue."

I started screaming because I couldn't help it. I was jumping up and down, and honestly, I guess it was everything. Landing the *SI* cover, being back in the modeling game, knowing that I'd beat Savannah Hughes's scrawny butt out of a job. I know the last thing isn't an especially nice thing to say. But honestly, didn't she deserve it?

"The *SI* team really loved your backstory," Leslie said. "In fact, I do believe you'll be a first in two categories. Their first plus-size model and their first model from the Ivy Leagues. The shoot is in two weeks, so I hate to say it, darling, but it's diet time. It's swimsuit, and you're representing for all the plus-size girls out there. I want no bloating and super-toned."

"No problem," I said. Like I said, if I couldn't have a six-pack, I'd happily take a two-pack.

"I've stepped up your sessions with Jenisa for four hours a day," Leslie said. "You'll meet with her from five to seven in the morning and from six to eight every night. I trust you'll work this out with your professors."

"No problem," I repeated. It was the end of the term, and all we had to do was prep for exams. I say, "all we had to do" as if it were some easy thing, but I'd learned a lot about multitasking in the past few months. I'd get my work done.

"Okay, very good. The shoot is in Tulum, Mexico, which I hear is just stunning, and you're going to have an excellent time. Congratulations, Bee, you've earned it," Leslie said.

I took a deep breath. "Leslie, I really want to bring a friend with me," I said.

I could hear her pursing her lips over the phone. "Bee, we've talked about this. Modeling is a business. We do not bring along our friends. Didn't you learn anything from that three-hundred-thousand-dollar disaster your boyfriend caused?"

"Ex-boyfriend," I mumbled. "It's my friend, Chela. She's Latina, and if it wasn't for her, I wouldn't have had the courage to come to your office that day," I said. "A trip like this would mean the world to her."

There was a long silence on the other end of the phone. The kind of icy pause my mother gives when I ask her if she would get me something non-poncho-related for my birthday, which, by the way, is only two weeks away. In fact, I'd be celebrating it in Mexico on the *SI* shoot. How sweet was that?

"Hello, Leslie?" I asked, wondering if she'd put me on hold and forgotten about me.

"Very well," she said. "You can bring your friend. We'll even cover her expenses. But if she comes anywhere near the set or interferes in any way—"

"Got it," I said. "Loud and clear."

* * *

Now it was my turn to stalk Chela. I walked over to her apartment and rang the doorbell.

"Who is it?" she hollered through the intercom.

"Bee," I hollered back.

"I'm not home!" she screamed down.

"Come on, Chela, buzz me up," I said. "I came to eat crow and kiss up."

The front door to the building buzzed open.

"Well, when you put it that way," she said as she opened the front door to her apartment. She lived in a quad with three other suite mates. One of them, the one we called the Human Hole because she had so many piercings, was sitting in the living room blasting some kind of alternative rock.

"*Hola*, Hole," Chela said. I was kinda shocked that she would call the girl this to her face, but it was clear that her hearing was severely impaired.

"A LITTLE PRIVACY!" Chela screamed.

The Human Hole turned down the music and went into her own room. "I can hear perfectly fine," she groused. "You don't have to shout."

I sat down on the couch, but Chela wasn't having it.

"I didn't say you could sit," she said, swiveling her neck as if she were telling a particularly cruel yo-mama joke.

"Look, I'm sorry. I screwed up. Brian had me all confused, and I thought I was in love. Then all this modeling stuff happened, and I didn't know how to act; I mean, I've never been a model before. I didn't mean to treat you like you were some sort of plebeian. You're my best friend and I want to make up."

Chela sucked her teeth and put her hand on her hip. "Let me think about it."

I said, "Can you think quick? Because I've got this crazy-sweet photo shoot in Tulum, Mexico, in two weeks, and I want to take you with me, but I have to book your tickets today."

She looked really serious and started swivel necking all over again. "See, Bee, this is why you and me can't hang anymore. You can't just buy my friendship like that. . . ."

Then she burst out laughing. "I'm just joking. Tulum? Are you serious? I'm in."

"Excellent," I said. "Can I sit down now?"

And while the Human Hole tried to turn the whole building deaf with her music, we sat on the couch and caught up on our lives—book, chapter, and verse.

* * *

Two weeks later, Chela and I were in front of my building waiting for the town car to pick us up. She was wearing some vintage Bianca Jagger–style jumpsuit that I swear only skinny girls can get away with. I was wearing my favorite Matthew Williamson sundress and a cardigan. I had on cute shoes, but I'd tucked a pair of flip-flops inside my Jimmy Choo tote bag in case it was a long trip and I needed to give in to the need for comfort. The town car pulled up.

The driver came out of the car and said, "Ms. Chesterfield wants to make sure you have your passport with you."

Of course I did.

"Just double-check," Chela said as she pulled out hers.

I rummaged through my bag. No passport. I ran back upstairs to get it.

What was that mess I was talking about my greatest asset being my brain?

Inside the terminals, Chela went off to the bookstore to get us a stack of magazines and two copies of the new Lisa Scottoline mystery to keep us occupied on the plane. I had popped into the bathroom when I realized there was a girl hot on my heels; she almost followed me into the stall! I turned around. She was around my age, but her hair was cut in this awkward cut that made it look like a duck's bottom. She was a few sizes bigger than me. I'd guess she was a size eighteen. But I'd also guess that the clothes she was wearing were a size twenty-two.

"Hi, can I help you?" I asked.

"Are you one of those Trophy Life girls?" she said.

"Yes," I said.

"You're my idol. I mean, all of you are my idols. I work in the concession stand here, and as soon as I save up enough money, I'm going to go to modeling school so I can be a plus-size model too."

I sighed. Who was I to dash her dreams? But she was five foot two. The chances of her becoming a plus-size model were not good, not good at all. Not to mention, Leslie had told me dozens of horror stories about modeling schools and other places that take your money in order to get you into the business.

"You should never pay someone to get you into modeling," I said. "But I'm wondering, why do you want to be a model?"

The girl looked down at her shoes. "So people will stop calling me fat," she said.

I lifted her chin and then told her the sad truth. "People still call me fat. My best friend called me fat just a few weeks ago. Being a model isn't going to stop people from being mean to you. In some ways, it just makes you more vulnerable."

"But you're famous. I see you everywhere, on TV and in magazines and on billboards. It must feel good to see your face everywhere."

I couldn't lie; it did. But I wondered, "Before you wanted to be a model, what did you want to be?"

"I wanted to be a travel agent," she said. "That's why I got a job at the airport. I love to be near planes. Even if I don't go anywhere, it makes me happy."

"Then you should look into that," I said. "Your life starts now. Not five pounds from now."

She had tears in her eyes and said, "Could I give you a hug?"

I said okay and hugged her.

"Now if you'll excuse me, I really, really have to pee," I said.

I went into the stall and thought—what a strange thing. I'd had an entire conversation with that girl, about her hopes and dreams and fears, and I didn't even know her name.

* * *

When we got to the resort, it turned out that it wasn't a traditional hotel. We would all be sleeping in these little *palapas* on the beach. Chela and I had one all to ourselves. So many people I knew were there. Melody, while not on the cover, would be featured in the magazine, and both Andy and Syreeta would be doing my hair and makeup.

Every morning, at five A.M., Melody led us all in a yoga

class on the beach. We were in hair and makeup at six, started shooting at eight, then worked until two P.M., when the sun made it too hot to continue.

Every afternoon at four, Chela and I had surf lessons. Which was, as you can imagine, pretty funny. Chela kept popping up too soon. And I kept paddling out too long. But it was so cool.

The last night of the shoot was my birthday, and all day long, nobody said anything. So I thought, You know what? No biggie. I'm in Mexico, modeling these fabulous swimsuits, hanging with two of my best friends, and having a great time. That night, Chela and I were finally going to do some dancing; my early call time had kept me from going out any of the other nights.

Chela wore this floral-print Roberto Cavalli dress that the stylist had given her, and I wore a long Caribbean blue dress I'd bought from J. Crew. We both decided to go barefoot since we'd walk along the beach from our *palapa* to the hotel restaurant and bar.

The bar overlooked the pool, and there were like a hundred tin Mexican lanterns hanging above the bar, all throwing off different-colored light. When we got there, it was strangely quiet. Then I heard a very familiar voice call out, "Happy birthday, Beatrice!"

It was Leslie, who must've flown in special for the occasion, Melody, and the whole photo crew. There was a long table in the restaurant set for twenty and an orchid on every plate.

Before we sat down, Doug, the photographer, handed me a gigantic box to unwrap. Inside, there was a hot pink surfboard signed by the whole *Sports Illustrated* team.

"Congratulations, Bee," Doug said, giving me the fashion two-cheek kiss. "It's rare in this industry to find such a combination of brains and beauty. You've got a bright future ahead of you."

"I'd like to toast to that," Leslie said, raising her glass.

"Salud!" Chela called out.

"Salud!" we all answered back as we clinked glasses.

At the end of the evening, after dinner and a round of margaritas, the waiters brought out a cake with eighteen candles. I blew them out, but I have to tell you a secret. For the first time I didn't wish for a thing, not for a pair of the latest hot jeans or for a boy to like me back, nothing — except for the good sense to know how lucky I was and to appreciate each and every otherworldly moment that being a model threw my way.

27

Bee-loved

I didn't think anything could top the *Sports Illustrated* shoot, but the week after we got back, Leslie called to say that I'd been chosen to host the Teen Choice Awards.

It was my first time hosting an awards show, but the rehearsals had gone well and, as Leslie liked to remind me, it doesn't take a college degree to read a teleprompter. Although I have to say, it's a whole lot harder than it looked.

I had my outfit picked out for the show: an Alice and Olivia minidress because I figured it was a teen thing, not a fashion thing. It was funny. I was technically still a teen, but I felt much, much older.

That morning, when the doorbell rang, I almost didn't bother to answer it since I wasn't expecting anyone. Andy and Syreeta were going to meet me at Lincoln Center to do my hair and makeup there. When I buzzed the intercom, I heard, "It's Chela; I was in the neighborhood. Let me in."

I'm here to tell you that while being a supe is a pretty amazing thing, getting your best friend back after a big tuss up is even better. I love my modeling friends, but I love that Chela's not part of that world and that she was my pal way before anyone ever put me on the cover of a magazine.

When I opened the front door to my apartment, I could hear a gaggle of noise making its way toward me. Maybe Chela's sisters were in town again. She had like five sisters, and wherever the crew of them went, it was a party. I got up, still dressed in my BedHead I Love Lucy pajamas, and saw that Chela was there. But she didn't have her sisters with her, she had the Trophy Life girls in tow: Melody, Prageeta, and Elsie.

"What are you doing here?" I asked, hugging Prageeta first.

"Hanif had a meeting with his American publisher, so I decided to come over and see my friends," she said.

"Oh, this is cute," Elsie said, examining my pajamas. "Not at all sexy, but cute."

"What are you guys doing here?" I asked, wiping the sleep out of my eyes. "It's so early."

Melody laughed. "Now we know you're a supermodel. It's not early; it's almost eleven o'clock."

I looked over at my CD alarm clock; why hadn't Snoop and Pharrell woken me up? Then I remembered that I'd been up so late studying for my physics final that I'd fallen asleep without setting the alarm.

"Okay, right," I said. "I mean, it's nice to see you, but what are you guys all doing here? Are we going to brunch? Did we make a date?"

Chela grabbed me by the arm. "No, we're not going to brunch; we've brought brunch to you."

Melody held up four shopping bags from our favorite brunch spot. "We got all your favorites: pumpkin waffles, the almond-crusted French toast, the four-flowers juice."

It was like some sort of a dream. All the girls coming to see me, my favorite foods, nowhere to go, and nothing to do until the awards show that night. They were all crowded around my room, and I thought, This is what I always imagined college to be like—hanging out with a posse of smart, worldly girls.

"But Sarabeth's doesn't do takeout," I said, my mouth full with the heavenly taste of a cheese blintz.

Prageeta gave me her biggest megawatt grin. "They don't do takeout for civilians. But we're models, darling."

Chela said in a mock-hurt voice, "Hey, I'm not a model."

Melody said, "That's okay; you still get perks."

We had moved into the dining room so that we could eat on proper plates and use cutlery. (We had begun to tear apart the pumpkin waffles with our bare hands in my utensil-free room.) Luckily, with four suite mates, the apartment was outfitted with enough chairs and a table big enough to accommodate our feast.

"This is great," I said, knocking back the rest of my delicious four-flowers juice. The only thing that was wrong with it was, unlike the ice tea, they never gave free refills of juice. "The Teen Choice Awards are going to have to be pretty great to top this."

"Well, since you mention it," Chela said, breaking into a freestyle beat box. "That's why we're here."

"Meaning?" I was beginning to get a little nervous.

"We're going to give you a makeover," Elsie said.

I looked down at my I Love Lucy pajamas and tugged a strand of my greasy hair. "What? It's not like I plan on going out looking like this."

"We know, *niña*," Chela said, putting her arm around my shoulders. "We just want to make sure that when that show goes on live tonight, you look like the supe that you are."

* * *

Chela and the Trophy Life girls had put together a whole day of beauty for me.

"To start with, I think it would be good if you took a shower," Elsie said, pretending to hold her nose.

"Take a bath," Melody said. "While you're in there, you can read this month's *Yoga Journal*." She reached into her bag, a very cute, very covetable Yves Saint Laurent Muse bag, and handed me the magazine.

"Thanks," I said, checking it out. I loved taking yoga classes with Melody and was convinced that they were keeping me sane.

"Think peaceful thoughts," Melody said.

I ran a bath and read a couple of the articles in Melody's magazine while soaking in the tub. I threw on a Four Seasons terry cloth robe, a gift from Leslie, and walked down the hallway into the living room. The simple Ikea-style living room had been transformed into a fashion-shoot dressing room. I'd heard the racket, but I assumed it was Chela and Elsie showing everyone the latest reggaeton moves.

There were literally racks of clothes and shoes and accessories. Moreover, Andy and Syreeta had joined the crowd. Andy had laid out his hair tools all over the dining-room table. Syreeta had commandeered a desk and turned it into a makeup station.

Melody was putting out platters of fresh fruit on the coffee table, and there were two champagne buckets filled with ice, sparkling water, and fruit spritzers.

"This is unbelievable," I said, fighting the urge to pinch myself. It was one thing to get the full glamour-gal treatment at work and quite another to get it in your own apartment.

"When we said we'd hook you up. . ." Elsie began.

"We meant we'd *hook you up*!" Chela said, finishing her sentence.

I could feel the tears coming, and I could barely get the words out. "Youguysarethebest," I said, everything I wanted to say tumbling out in a soppy jumble. "Idon't knowhowtothankyou.I'mtheluckiestgirlintheworld."

"Go ahead, girl," Syreeta said, putting her arm around

me. "Get it all out now. Because once I start doing makeup, you better not shed a single tear."

"Wardrobe first," Elsie said, leading me over to the racks of clothes.

"How did you guys get all of this stuff?" I asked. "It's like I died and went to Bergdorf's heaven."

"We've got friends in stylish places," Elsie quipped. "Now what were you planning on wearing?"

I went to my room and came back with the Alice and Olivia dress. She held it up and gave it the once-over.

"It's cute, but I think you don't want to look like you're trying too hard," Melody said, pulling out a pair of jeans. "I think you should wear these and a silky halter top."

"Okay, that's a look," Elsie said. "Let's pull some shoes to try on with that."

Melody went over to the shoe area and picked up a pair of four-inch Sergio Rossi gold heels. She laid it all out on the sofa.

"Great, that's look number one," Elsie said, taking on the role of ringleader/chief fashion diva with pleasure and ease. "Chela, what do you think?"

"I think Bee does preppy so well," Chela said, pulling out an emerald green J. Crew silk-taffeta skirt and a hot pink cashmere cardigan with a jeweled neckline.

"Good job, Chela, that's look number two," Elsie said.

"I LOVE that," I said. "Can I buy that to keep?"

"We'll hook you up, promise," Elsie said. "But time is

flying, and we need to make sure we get all the looks together before we decide what you'll wear. And, of course,
Andy and Syreeta can't decide on hair and makeup until
you've picked an outfit. So Chela, choose."

Chela walked over to the shoes and chose a really sweet
pair of ballet flats.

"No way," Prageeta said. "She can't wear flats."

"Why not?" Chela said.

"Because she's a supe. She's gotta give them glamazon
Amazon. These would be better."

Prageeta handed Chela a pair of high-heeled patent-
leather Mary Janes.

Chela looked them over. "These will work."

Elsie said, "Okay, London girl, your turn."

Prageeta said, "I think Bee is so unique, so un-model–
like, that she should do something that reflects more of her
independent spirit. That's why I asked my friend at De-
cades in L.A. to send me this vintage Anna Sui dress."

She pulled out a sleeveless black dress with a ruffled
white bib front. It was cool in that Austin-Powers-London-
in-the-sixties kind of way. It was the kind of dress that I
always dream about wearing in a photo shoot: something
so graphic and clean that it's almost more like a piece of
architecture than a dress.

"That's gorgeous," I said.

Everyone agreed; there were murmurs of approval
all around. Trust Prageeta to find something you couldn't

even get in a regular store.

"It's hot," said Elsie. "That's look number four."

"What are you thinking about for shoes?" I asked.

Prageeta pulled out a pair of thigh-high patent-leather black boots. "Aren't these funky?" she said.

"They are. And so will my feet be if I wear thigh-high boots in the summer!" I said.

Prageeta rolled her eyes.

"I know, I know," I said. "You've got to suffer for beauty."

Elsie was the only one who hadn't chosen.

"So Elsie, what do you have in mind?" I asked.

"I was thinking about how much you're always talking about your agent, Leslie, and how impeccable she always looks," Elsie said, pulling out a simple sheath dress. "I think you should channel some of that tonight. Do a bit of a Park Avenue princess."

"Shoes?" Melody asked.

"Black Louboutins. Simple black clutch," Elsie said, pulling out the matching items.

"Nice," Melody said. "Really nice."

I gazed over at the different "looks" my friends had pulled for me: 1940s movie star. Rock-star casual. Country-club cool. Austin Powers mod. Park Avenue princess.

I loved them all, and I had a ball trying them on. Chela was playing DJ, and hip hop, salsa, and reggaeton blared through the apartment. I pretended my hallway was a runway, and I strutted my stuff, not the way Savannah Hughes would do it, but the way I did it, in each and every outfit. "Do *you*," Chela was always saying. As I tried on each outfit that my friends had picked for me with love and affection, I did *me* — and it felt good.

The minute I slipped on the dress Elsie had picked, I knew it was the one. The top of the dress was leaf green; the bottom half was a solid navy block. It was like a Rothko painting, and it felt so comfortable.

I walked down the hallway putting a little extra "sashay, Shantay" into my walk. When I got to the living room, all the girls started hooting and hollering.

"That's fabulous," Melody said.

"I want it," Prageeta said, which was her way of saying the same thing.

"That dress puts a little sauce into her walk," Chela said, nudging Melody with her elbow. "Did you notice how she walked out here like a girl who just got some? Now, that's how you host a television awards show."

"It's good," Elsie said.

"It's better than good," I said, giving her a big hug. "It's the one."

Elsie asked Andy to sweep my hair into a high ponytail. Then, to give it some extra vavoom, he attached a hairpiece — an extra-long ponytail that made it seem like my hair hit the top of my butt.

Syreeta did my makeup — really soft cheeks and lips,

but superbright blue-and-green eyes and pink, glossy lips.

Chela even did my nails in a color that Elsie had picked, although she said, "It's killing me to paint them in this boring clear shade."

"It's not clear," Elsie said. "It's ballet pink."

Chela swiveled her neck. "I guess that's why I don't like the ballet. Ballet pink is boring pink."

By the time I was sitting back and enjoying my manicure, it was after six o'clock. Where did the day go? I wondered. Then I remembered: It didn't go, it flew because I was hanging with my *real* best friends.

* * *

The Teen Choice Awards were a blast. It seemed like every star I'd ever seen in a music video or in a movie or a TV show was there. It was really hard not to geek out backstage, but when I was onstage, all I had to do was look in the fifth row and see my mom, my dad, and my aunt Zo smiling up at me and I felt mega-calm again. Sometimes, when you're in a huge auditorium like Lincoln Center, you can get something known as crowd blindness and you can't make out specific faces in the crowd. But my mother was wearing this ginormous hand-beaded Zulu headdress that not for nothing was totally blocking Jessica Simpson's view. So my family was pretty easy to spot.

Even though we stopped for commercial breaks and the tech guys were constantly adjusting lights and mikes and sets for the musical numbers, the evening flew by so quickly. Before I knew it, I was giving out the last award, for best kiss.

I looked at the teleprompter to read the nominees. But instead of the list of names that had rolled during rehearsal, the prompter just said, "Enter DJ Drop and Roll."

I turned to the left of me and there was Kevin. He was wearing this really sharp black suit with a bright yellow shirt, and he had a mike in his hand.

I looked in the third row, and I could see that Melody, Elsie, and Chela were stomping their feet and screaming. All of a sudden, the day of beauty they'd given me had a much bigger purpose than just hosting the award show.

He was walking toward me, and I felt that fluttery, butterfly feeling like when you think a boy likes you and you *know* you like him, but you're not really 100 percent sure of anything.

"Y'all know who it is. DJ Drop and—" Kevin prompted the audience.

"Roll," they screamed back.

"I didn't hear you. DJ Drop and—"

"Roll," the auditorium screamed.

"Y'all like my outfit?" he asked the crowd. "I'm dressed in the colors of my favorite Bee," he said, putting his arm around me. Then he started to rap ABOUT ME. Right there. On live national TV.

He said:

"DJ Kev's on fire, but baby girl brings the heat.
Since the first day of class, honey dip was sweet.
Then she got into modeling and blew up the spot.
Love them curves and them swerves,
Man, y'all know she is hot.
We done had some beef, but I'm gonna put it to rest.
I've been waiting too long to put my love to the test."

Then he kissed me. Right there. On live national TV. Even though all those people (including my parents, I mean REALLY) were watching, I didn't feel embarrassed or awkward, like which way would I turn my nose and what happens if one of us slobbers too much. At the risk of sounding too corny, it was like our lips were made for each other's and I realized that I'd been wanting to kiss him for a very long time. We even took home the evening's last trophy. The Teen Choice Award for Best Kiss: Bee Wilson and Kevin Dean.

I do kind of worry that it's all downhill from here. I mean, not for nothing: It kind of puts a lot of pressure on that second kiss when your first kiss with a guy is seen by fifty million people nationwide and wins an award and stuff. But as Chela would say, "These are high-class problems." I'll cross that bridge, I mean that kiss, when I get there.